PHYSICS & THE HUMAN HEART

Short stories

Corie Ralston

Physics and the Human Heart

Copyright © 2021 by Corie Ralston

The stories in this collection are works of fiction. Names, characters, businesses, organizations, places, events and incidents either are the product of the author's imagination or are used fictitiously.

Cover design by Hugh Cowling

First Edition: July 2021

Contents

Quantum Entanglement

My father told us about the cat when I was eleven and Emma was six. He said Schrodinger did an experiment: he put a cat in a box with a vial of poison. If the vial broke, the cat was dead. If it didn't break, the cat was alive.

"What was the cat's name?" Emma asked. She twirled Teddy around by his arms. His round ears grazed the edge of the kitchen table where our father sat holding open a physics text.

I stood next to Emma. The window above the sink was open, and I heard jays calling to each other in the dry grass of our backyard.

"That isn't important," my father said. "The point is that the cat is both alive and dead at the same time." He raised one bushy eyebrow and smiled. His ears moved when he smiled, pulling his thick-framed glasses further up on his nose.

"I'd like a cat," Emma said. She held Teddy close to her chest.

"How can it be both alive and dead?" I asked. I was learning algebra in school, but my father liked to jump ahead. He had already taught me how to count in base two, and about the square root of negative numbers. He said I was the smartest girl in my class.

"Because there's no observer," my father said. "Schrodinger said that as long as there is no observer, the system exists in all its possibilities at once."

"But what about the cat?" Emma said. "Did he die?"

"That's not the point!" My father placed both hands on the table and pushed himself up, his chair scraping backwards over the linoleum. He picked up the book and walked from the kitchen.

We heard the door to his study slam shut.

The corner of Emma's mouth twitched.

"The cat was just fine," I told her. "His name was Bailey."

*

In my dream Bailey is still young, at that awkward stage between kitten and adult cat, paws and ears too large for his skinny frame. He winds around the base of my chair two times, but when I reach down to pet him, he is suddenly lying on his side, not breathing. His mouth opens, and a shrill cry emerges.

I wake from the dream with a start. It takes me a moment to realize my phone is ringing. The dream images recede, and the shadowy lumps on my floor resolve into books and clothes and stacks of journal articles. I pick up the phone.

"Judith," a voice says in my ear.

It takes me a moment to figure out it is Emma's voice on the phone.

"My god," I say. "Where are you?" I sit up and disentangle the blanket that has managed to wrap itself around my feet.

"Back in town. It's Tuesday. Math night." I can almost hear her cringe. "Were you studying?"

"Actually, I was asleep."

"I thought you would be up," she says.

I squint at the clock. Almost two in the morning.

"Not this week," I say. "I have to get enough sleep for my candidacy exam."

"Dad told me you were studying for something."

"You talked to him?" That's a conversation I can't imagine.

"Long enough to get your number."

I realize the line has a periodic hum to it. Voices rise and fall in the background. "Where are you staying?" I ask.

"I'm at the hospital," she says.

I pull the phone closer. "The hospital?" I say. "Are you okay?"

"Sure," she answers, too fast. "It's the impurities that cause problems, you know. Heroin isn't the problem. It's the fentanyl."

Heroin. Fentanyl. I don't know what to say. I reach over to the window and open it a crack. The city murmurs in its sleep. Cool air tickles the hair at the back of my neck.

I want to ask where she's been in the years she has been gone, what has happened, but I don't know where to start.

"I'm going into a detox program," she says. "They have a good one at the clinic downtown."

"That's great," I say. "Good for you."

"Dad says he's too busy to give me a ride to the clinic tomorrow."

The image comes to me of her standing in our driveway the morning she left. Someone had been with her. "What about your boyfriend?" I ask. "Blake."

"Blake?" She lets out a sound that is somewhere between a laugh and a snort. "He's long gone."

"Oh. I'm sorry."

"No loss," she says, and then is quiet.

I look around my apartment. Through the doorway to the kitchen I can see the silhouettes of plates and bowls protruding from the sink, and the small table that serves as an alternate bookcase. One more day, and then I can get my life in order again. I can't possibly take any time off until after the exam.

"Tomorrow morning I'm practicing with Dad," I say. "And in the afternoon is the exam."

She doesn't answer.

"Emma, this test is everything. It's what determines whether I get my degree or not."

"That's what I thought."

"It's not that I don't want to see you."

"Sure."

"I just can't tomorrow. I'm sorry. I'll come the day after."

"Okay. It's fine. Really. I'll take a bus."

I copy down the number for the clinic on a yellow stick-it. There is a soft click, and the dial tone hums in my ear.

*

We always waited together after school for our father, standing quietly on the strip of grass separating the sidewalk from the street. That day when our father pulled up in his silver Volvo, I touched the front door before Emma, and got dibs on the front seat.

I slid in and pulled the door shut behind me, grinning through the window at Emma.

She pounded a fist on my window, then stopped abruptly when she saw the cardboard box on the back seat.

A soft meowling emerged from the box.

I twisted around in my seat to look while she opened the lid.

The kitten fit entirely in her two cupped hands. He was all black except for one tiny white paw. His head wobbled back and forth a little, as if he were dizzy.

"Bailey," my sister whispered. She stroked the top of his head with one finger. He settled down in her hands, his head on his paws.

"You have to make sure he always has fresh water." My father watched Emma in the rear view mirror. "And you have to feed him every day, otherwise I'll take him back to the shelter."

Emma nodded. She held Bailey to her cheek.

"Put him away now," my father said.

She set him carefully back in the box, on top of the wadded paper towels, and we headed home.

*

For the fifth day in a row, I am going through a practice exam with my father. He sits at the back of the conference table and calls out questions while I stand in front of the whiteboard. He cannot, of course, sit on my candidacy committee, but he helped me pick out the members. I am their only female candidate this year, and the daughter of my father. I must not fail.

"What about the Uncertainty Principle?" he says.

From where I stand I can't see his eyes because of the glare on his glasses. Sunlight streams in through the blinds, leaving horizontal bands across the scratched oak table and tiled floor.

"Heisenberg said you can't measure certain properties of a system simultaneously with the same precision," I say. "Momentum and position, for instance." I write out the equation on the board.

"And why not?" he says.

"Dad. I got a call from Emma last night."

His lips tighten to a thin line. "Judith, you must concentrate."

"But I'm worried about her."

My father stands up and moves to the front of the room.

"First she flunks out of school," he says, holding up his index finger. "Then she runs off." Another finger. "And now she has appeared out of nowhere, and expects us to drop everything to take care of her." He makes a fist. "You should know better than to play her games."

I look at the marker in my hand. Maybe I should know better.

"Now," he says. He returns to his seat. "Why can't we measure these properties with precision?"

Heisenberg's analogy was that of trying to measure the position of a chandelier in the dark by swinging a broomstick. You always move the chandelier just by trying to figure out where it is.

"Because the observer is always part of the system," I say. "Whether she wants to be or not."

*

I watched my father pour hot water from the pan into the sink, the steam rising in puffy clouds around his face. When he turned back to the table, his face was red. I saw little beads of water on his forehead.

He rolled the hotdogs from the pan into the bowl in the middle of the table. I speared one onto my plate.

Bailey took his place behind Emma's chair, eyeing the food on the table.

"Now," my father said. He let himself sink into the chair between me and my sister. "What did we learn in school today?"

Emma was balancing her fork on the tip of her finger. She tapped the tines, making it rock like a see-saw.

"Nothing," she said.

"Nothing?" My father raised his eyebrows in mock surprise. "You mean the fifth grade doesn't teach anything any more? That's a fine use of my tax dollars."

The fork rocked back and forth. I concentrated on squeezing the ketchup onto my plate.

"We played cops and robbers," she said.

My father swept his hand across the table and Emma's fork and plate slid off with a clatter. The plate broke against the linoleum. Bailey dashed from the room.

For a moment, there was nothing but the sound of the clock ticking.

He said, "You will not eat dinner again until this behavior stops."

My sister stared straight ahead. She didn't blink.

"Judith," my father said. "What did you learn in school today?"

I chewed quickly and swallowed. I told him about the Pythagorean theorem, and then about how we had learned to use a quadrant. He told me about the Fibonacci series, how each two numbers adds up to the next one.

*

"You have all your slides?" It's the third time my father has asked the question on our walk through the campus. He rubs his thumb back and forth across his cheek.

I nod. The physics building is an old gray concrete block just beyond the little stream. We pause on the wooden bridge, elbows on the railing. Twenty minutes until the exam. I hold my laptop to my chest.

"Try to derive what you don't remember. They want to see that you can think things through, not that you can memorize facts."

I nod again. The water beneath us divides around a rock, coming together on the other side again. Waves overlap each other in ripples, an interference pattern.

"They'll ask you about the basics as well as current theory. Wave-particle duality. That sort of thing."

"I better go," I say.

My father squares his shoulders. "You'll do fine," he says.

I start to walk toward the concrete building. I can't stop

thinking about Emma. She will leave the hospital soon, head for the clinic. I almost turn to my father to tell him to call her, but I know what he would say. Concentrate. Tell me about wave-particle duality.

I keep walking.

I answer his question in my mind as I walk. Photons can be seen as either particles or waves, I tell him. Two identical photons behave entirely differently depending on how they are looked at.

*

It was Wednesday, language night.

My sister and I were sitting next to each other on the small couch, facing our father, who was in his leather chair by the bookcase. The hardwood floor of his study smelled of lemon oil, a smell I associated with evening study sessions.

"Judith will start," he said. He opened the dictionary, ran his finger down the tissue-thin page.

"Cobble," he said.

"To repair or make," I said.

He turned the page. "Coddle. Emma?"

My sister sat on the edge of the couch, swinging her legs back and forth. She tucked her chin to her chest and mumbled something.

"What was that?" my father said. "Speak up."

"I don't know." She watched a spot on the carpet intently.

"It means to pamper," he said. "Now you know. Okay?"

"Okay. How did Mom die?"

My father's hands tightened on the edges of the dictionary. "She got very sick."

Her legs stopped swinging and she looked up at the picture on the bookcase behind our father's chair. Our mother smiled out at us from the photograph. I couldn't see her eyes because the upper half of her face was in shadow from a floppy wide-brimmed hat. Dad had already told me it was cancer, and that she decided to take some pills rather than die slowly for years. But we couldn't tell Emma yet because she wouldn't understand.

Our father cleared his throat. He looked at the page. "Judith. Coruscating."

"Sparkling," I said.

"Crass. Emma?"

She started swinging her legs even harder than before, and her heel caught the hem of my new skirt.

"Stop it!" I said.

"Settle down, Emma," my father said.

She jumped up and ran from the room.

My father shook his head. "She'll never learn. She can't sit still." He closed the dictionary. "We'll move on to geometry."

I liked math better than language, anyway. My father said Mom had been a professor of math, and that's how he met her, since the math and physics departments were in the same building at the university. He said I would be a physicist, too. I was twelve, then, but he said I was already thinking like a scientist.

*

I am standing in front of the committee, five men in button-down oxfords around the oak conference table. Equations cover the board behind me. My hands are sweaty and my throat is dry.

"Tell us about quantum entanglement," Prof. Erickson says. He has a semicircle of gray hair around his head, and a huge beard that he smoothes as he speaks.

"It has to do with the way particles are linked," I say. "The properties of particles can be correlated, or entangled. Properties like spin, position, or momentum."

He nods, his face cryptic. He tugs at his beard. "So?" he says. "What is the significance of it?"

They are all watching me silently.

I swallow. I feel an urgent need to use the bathroom, though I was careful to go right before the start of the examination two hours ago. I think of Emma, suddenly, standing in front of my father's chair, parroting what her teachers had said in order to eat dinner.

"Well?" Professor Erickson sits forward.

I force my thoughts on the question.

"It means that two particles that have once interacted are forever linked. They influence each other instantaneously and over large distances." It makes no sense, I almost add, then stop myself. How can one particle's behavior affect another if they are so far apart?

*

I was woken abruptly that night by a brush of cold air across my ankles. Light spilled through my half-open door.

I got up and moved into the hall. The light came from my sister's room. Through her door I could see clothes and shoes and bottles of nail polish strewn across her bed. Emma was just coming in through the window.

She saw me, one leg thrown over the sill. She paused, then pulled the other leg through and jumped into the room. She wore frayed jeans, a tank top, and heavy black eyeliner.

"What the fuck are you looking at?" she said. The word 'fuck' was a recent addition to her vocabulary. She was twelve. Her new boyfriend Georgio put needles through his earlobes and gelled his hair so it stuck straight up.

"Nothing," I said. "Where did you go?"

"None of your business." She began to peel off her tank top. She was wearing a bra, though she didn't need one yet. "You planning on telling Daddy?"

The eyeliner and eyeshadow were so dark her eyes looked like bruises when she stood with her back to the light.

I turned and went back to my room. I had just sent out my college applications. I was praying that I got into Stanford, though Cal Tech would be acceptable as well.

*

Indistinct voices rise and fall within the conference room where the committee is deciding my fate. I stand with my back against the dark wood paneling of the hallway, facing the closed door.

I check my watch. Almost four. If they finish soon, I'll have time to go to the clinic before I call my father.

Footsteps echo from the staircase at the far end of the hall. Jacob, a fifth-year, approaches. His hair is a bush of tangled curls, imitation-Einstein. Rumor has it his advisor changed his dissertation project twice already, and he will never finish. He asked me out when I first started graduate school. Since I said no, he hasn't spoken to me except as necessary at department parties.

"Waiting is the hardest part," he says.

I allow him a small smile.

"Don't worry. You'll pass." He runs a finger down his nose. "It would look pretty bad if they failed the daughter of the chair."

I meet his gaze without comment. I have lots of practice at this sort of thing.

Finally, Jacob smiles and walks on. I rub the palms of my hands on my slacks.

Watching Jacob's retreating back, I get a sudden sense of vertigo, as if he is standing still and I am the one moving away. It is like the twin paradox: according to relativity, you can't tell who is actually moving. The twin on the spaceship sees the earth and all the people on it racing away at near the speed of light.

Each twin thinks the other is abandoning her.

*

I was up late that night, almost through with my calculus homework, when I heard Bailey meowing. I got up and peered down the hallway. The door to my sister's room was closed.

He let out another cry, and I realized it was coming from outside. I went to the front door and opened it, letting in the damp night air.

Bailey was in his carrier on the driveway. In the moonlight I could see only the glint from his eyes and his one white paw within the carrier. Emma stood next to him, and on the other side was her large duffel bag. She was arguing in low whispers with Blake, her current boyfriend.

I turned on the porch light and stepped onto the front path, the cement cold beneath my bare feet.

Blake watched me approach.

"I told you we should have left already," he said. A bead necklace encircled his throat, and he wore a pullover with sleeves that were too long. The frayed ends came halfway over his wrists.

"What are you doing?" I said.

Emma turned. Her face was flushed, though she clasped her arms across her chest, shivering in her t-shirt. Her pupils were so large I could barely see the rim of brown at the edges.

"We're running away," she told me.

Blake moved to stand behind her, his hands on her shoulders.

"We're in love," she said.

Bailey pawed at the metal bars on the carrier door.

"You're not in love," I said.

"What do you know about love?" she asked.

She had a point. I had only had one boyfriend, and we never even kissed. We held hands a few times. His palms were always clammy, and the soap he used didn't completely cover the smell of something organic underneath, something animal, like the way Bailey's fur smelled when he had been outside in the sun all day. Math was more interesting than boys, anyway. It was clean and predictable, and it always made sense.

"You have to finish school," I said.

"Says who?" A smile stretched her face thin. "Dad? He doesn't care what I do."

Blake picked up the duffel in one hand and the carrier in the other. He held it at an angle, and Bailey slid to the back. I heard his claws scrabbling against the hard plastic.

"Let's go," he said.

"I wanted to say goodbye," Emma said. "But I can see you're in a bad mood."

I wanted to tell her she was wrong, that Dad did care, but I was suddenly not so sure.

She followed Blake to his battered Toyota. They put the duffel and Bailey in the back seat.

I watched the cloud of exhaust burst from the tailpipe,

and then they were gone. I went back inside to my homework.

*

The committee is still murmuring within the conference room. It's too hot in the building. I feel sweat on the small of my back. I hear my heart beating through my body, marking off the time until the clinic closes.

If I don't leave soon I will miss the visiting hours.

My heart ticks off another minute.

Something catches inside me, and I pick up my laptop and walk down the hall. When I push open the doors at the end of the hall, I can see the sky is overcast, a light rain just starting.

The cement path leads from the building toward the small creek that runs through campus. I pass over the small arched ridge and toward the edge of campus. The raindrops collect at the back of my neck and run down beneath the collar of my blouse. I begin to shiver.

I have passed the exam. I have failed. All possibilities exist until I know the result.

My apartment is on the street bordering the north edge of campus, where the tree-lined campus paths give way to noisy city streets. I open the door, nudging back the pile of books that has collapsed behind the door.

My blouse is soaked through, clinging to my shoulder blades.

I find the stick-it note with the phone number under a

book.

I give Emma's name to the woman who answers. "She was supposed to start the detox program today," I say.

I hear fingernails tapping against a keyboard. "Looks like she never showed up," the woman says.

"Never showed up?"

She lets out a sigh. "Half of them never show. More often than not they just head off to the streets again."

Not my sister, I think. She must still be at the hospital. But then the woman says, "Looks like she checked out of the hospital this morning at ten."

I hang up.

My head feels very light.

My sister is alive. She is dead. She is lying in a stairwell of an abandoned building on urine-stained steps, neck twisted at an impossible angle. She is walking calmly down Main street, looking for a job. She is sitting on a Greyhound bus, heading off for another city.

The phone rings. *Emma.*

But it's my father's voice on the line, not Emma's.

"Well?" he says. His question is filled with certainty. He knows I passed the exam. In his world, there is no other possibility.

"I don't know," I say.

"What?" I can hear his disbelief. "Didn't you pass?"

"I left before they told me."

"How could you just leave? I don't understand—"

"Did Emma call you?" I ask.

"Emma? No. Why?"

"She isn't at the hospital anymore. She checked out."

"And what on earth does that have to do with the exam?" His voice grows louder.

Nothing. Everything. I hang up.

The phone immediately rings again and I turn it off.

It is quiet in my apartment, and stuffy. The spider plant above the kitchen sink is beyond help, dead brown leaves sprouting from even drier soil.

I walk into all the rooms, open all the windows. The rain patters in, dotting the books and journal articles, bringing the smell of wet grass. Cars pass with a soft shush against damp pavement.

I realize I never found out what happened to Bailey. Maybe Emma gave him away. Maybe he died. I try to imagine him curled up somewhere on someone's wool blanket, listening to the rain tap against the window. He would be almost fifteen years old now. "I hope you made it," I say.

I walk out into the rain to search for Emma.

The Giving Heart

Coleman studied the dead heart in the store window, the aorta frozen mid-pump in clear acrylic.

Julie put a hand over her mouth. "Is this for real?"

"Sandra says it's all the rage," Coleman said. "It's what everyone is doing at weddings these days."

"Sandra says this, Sandra says that."

Coleman glanced over. Could it be she didn't want him to marry Sandra? He liked the thought.

He pulled Julie inside. A man in a suit approached them at once and held out a hand with perfect, manicured nails.

"Real is the new real," Mr. Manicured said. "People used to give chocolate hearts, candy hearts, paper hearts. Why not get to the heart of the matter, so to speak? Give your actual heart."

"I don't know," Julie said. "It's kind-of creepy."

"How does it work?" Coleman said.

Julie wandered off to a display kiosk and pulled up a graphic demo of heart-replacement surgery.

Coleman concentrated on Mr. Manicured, who was still speaking.

"Our surgeons are the best in the country," he said. "And with cutting edge surgical techniques, so to speak, there is practically no scarring."

A holo of a happy couple danced in the corner. Red slogans slid across the walls in laser light. *Home is where the heart is, give her your heart.* It all seemed very modern.

Mr. Manicured took Coleman's elbow and leaned in conspiratorially. "Personally," he said, "I would take an artificial heart over a real one any day. Much more reliable."

He named a price.

Coleman gasped.

"Do you love her?" Manicured said.

"Sure." It would take all his savings, the money he was saving for his bookstore.

"There is no cost too great for love," Manicured murmured.

Sandra said it was about time they get married. She sighed meaningfully whenever they passed the *Give Your Heart* store. He did want to make her happy.

Coleman looked over at Julie, who stood with eyes narrowed at the kiosk. Julie, on the other hand, didn't believe in marriage.

"I'll do it," he said.

*

"Do you, Coleman?" the minister said.

Coleman blinked. "What?"

Sandra's shimmery veil made him dizzy. The heat wrapped his head like a soggy towel. He could scarcely breathe.

"Here."

Sandra's nephew, at Coleman's side in his tiny tux, nudged a package into Coleman's hands.

"Do you, Coleman, take Sandra as your wife?"

He knew he was supposed to say something about his heart. *Still my beating heart. My heart is breaking?* No, that couldn't be it. There were so many expressions about the heart, he thought in a sudden panic.

Julie had said he shouldn't get married. Julie was somewhere in the audience.

After a pause that felt to Coleman as if it might stretch to eternity, Sandra reached over and took the package from Coleman's hands. The minister began to speak again.

Coleman felt a sudden thump from within his chest, as if his new artificial heart had done a somersault. The surgeon had assured him his new heart was in fine condition. Nothing could go wrong. So why had it thumped like that?

He knew he was now supposed to do something with the ring, but at that point, he lost consciousness.

*

No one would let him live down the fact that he had fainted; the reception was one long running joke about it. Coleman's heart, in its acrylic cage, made the rounds of the room.

Coleman drank three martinis and wobbled off to a corner where Sandra's brother Giles gobbled a piece of red heart-shaped cake.

"The problem with weddings these days," Giles said, since he was an expert on everything, "is that they are so staged and predictable."

"You mean fainting wasn't exciting enough for you?"

Giles laughed. "Okay. That was fun. But really, everything else. The dresses, the vows, the flowers, blah blah blah."

And Julie was there, all of a sudden. She looked at Giles. "They were all exotics," she said. "Not blah blah."

Giles smiled and held out his hand. "One thing is for sure. I would never cut my heart out and give it to someone."

"Good," Julie said, taking Giles's hand. "I would never ask anyone to. Have you seen Coleman's heart in the acrylic? It's quite gross."

Giles smiled at Julie. Coleman didn't like it. Julie smiled

at Giles. Coleman didn't like it one bit. The thought of all those expensive flowers weighed on Coleman and sapped all the bravado he had recently acquired through the martinis. He kept thinking that he could have spent that money on a really nice collection of books.

The thing in his chest thumped again, followed by a faint slithering sound.

"Did you hear that?" Coleman said.

"Hear what?" Julie said.

Coleman took a breath. "Nothing," he said. It was the stress of the day. The thought of all his savings now gone, and everyone staring at him all the time. He rubbed his temples and wondered if there was somewhere he could lie down.

"You don't look so good," Giles said.

"I feel great," Coleman said. "Best day of my life."

Giles shrugged.

"Really. I'm so happy." He thought maybe it was the alcohol that made his voice waver.

Julie put a hand on Coleman's shoulder. "Of course you are, Coleman. Congratulations."

I give you my life, my love, my heart. That's what he had been supposed to say.

*

"There! Did you see that?" Coleman said.

He stood with his shirt unbuttoned, holding open the flaps so Sandra could see.

The skin of his chest bulged out faintly, like a fast-growing blister, and then just as quickly smoothed out again.

"See what? Coleman, you aren't listening to me."

"I'm listening to you." Maybe he was imagining it. Sandra didn't see it, after all. "You said you can't stand living in the city."

"It's killing me," she said. "The endless rain. This apartment is so crowded. All those stupid books."

She lay on the couch with her arm draped over her eyes.

"We can't afford a house here," he said. "And what about my bookstore?"

"What bookstore?" she said. "We could afford a house in the suburbs."

Maybe it was just the idea of something alive in there that gave him chills. The sensation of something crawling around in his chest.

"I'm miserable here," she said. "Don't you care about that?"

"Of course I care," he said.

"Don't you love me?" she said.

"Of course I love you."

He loved his little apartment. He loved the proximity to bookstores and cafes, the ceaseless pattern of traffic alternately stopping and then pulsing forward like blood through veins. He loved the sound of the rain. And he would be so far from Julie.

"When do you want to move?" he said.

She finally lifted her arm, smiled. "I'll call an agent right now."

*

The tip of the thing poked out his nose, made a small circular motion, and then began to lengthen, sliding smoothly out, long and thin and dexterous.

Coleman wanted to scream but found he was completely frozen.

"Coleman?" Sandra's voice came from the kitchen. "Have you seen my keys?"

The thin tentacle patted the dining room table, poked under a pile of newspapers. Coleman breathed shallowly through his mouth. He hoped he would faint. Or wake up. This couldn't be happening.

The tentacle rooted under the newspapers, came out holding the ring of keys like an elephant trick at a circus. It rattled the keys in front of Coleman's face. He opened his hand, and the keys dropped into his palm. The tentacle slid smoothly back inside his nose.

Sandra appeared in the doorway.

"There they are!" She scooped the keys from Coleman's outstretched hand. "Everything is so hard to find. We really need to unpack."

The garage door slammed. Coleman still stood with his hand outstretched, unable to move.

*

"It does appear to be moving around." The doctor withdrew the probe from the small hole he had made in Coleman's belly-button. The local anesthetic didn't completely cover the sensation of cold metal slipping around inside him.

"Is this *normal*?" Coleman asked.

"Well, I've read about cases like this, although I haven't seen it personally. When you remove your real heart it leaves room for a different kind of creature to grow."

"A *creature*?"

"We can schedule you for surgery next week," he said.

Coleman tried to take deep breaths to calm himself. "Do you have any reading material on this phenomenon?"

"Sure. I'll send you home with some literature. You can think about how you want to proceed."

*

Sandra found him on the doorstep, duffel in hand.

"Where are you going?" she said.

"I hate this suburb," he said. "All the houses look identical. It never rains here."

"Are you *leaving* me?"

"I'm going to the hospital. And then I think I might go live in the city for a while."

"The hospital?"

"I have a thing growing inside me where my heart used to be," he said. "I'm going to have it surgically removed."

She gave him a blank look. He handed her the literature.

"This is very strange," she said finally.

"I'll see you later," he said.

"Wait a minute," she said. "It says in here the creature can often be very helpful."

"It's disgusting," Coleman said.

"And it says the insurance won't cover its removal."

"Sandra, I need to leave now to make my appointment."

"Just come inside for a moment and let's talk about it."

"What's to talk about?" he said. His hand on the duffel was sweating. "There's a fucking creature inside of me!"

"Calm down, Coleman." She glanced around to make sure no neighbors were out. "Really now." She leaned in close. "Did you see the cost of the surgery? We can't afford that."

"I don't care what it costs."

"You're being selfish. Are you going to take all our savings and spend it on yourself?"

"Well—"

"You aren't even thinking about how this might affect me. Remember how we agreed we would make our decisions together?"

He dropped the duffel. Sandra picked it up. "Come inside," she said. "We'll work this out."

The tentacle slid out of Coleman's ear and opened the door for Sandra.

"See?" she said. "It's just trying to help."

*

The creature was indeed very helpful. Tentacles protruded from Coleman's nose and mouth and pushed the vacuum cleaner around, did the dishes, found the remote. They picked up his old acrylic heart and put it on the mantel. They unpacked boxes, picked up his piles of dusty old books and dropped them in the recycle bin.

One night Sandra asked Coleman to make love to her, and he watched with a mixture of arousal and horror as a tentacle protruded from the tip of his penis and caressed her, brought her to climax. She made noises he hadn't heard in quite a while. When it was done, he was still aroused, but he didn't want to touch her. And anyway, she was already asleep.

The next morning he woke up to the smell of coffee and bacon. Sandra hung up the phone when he entered the kitchen, her eyes bright.

"Giles broke up with Julie." She shrugged. "About time. I never understood what he saw in her anyway."

She draped an arm over his shoulders, whispered in his ear. "But we're so happy, aren't we?"

"Hmmm," Coleman said. He opened the paper.

A tentacle emerged from his ear and caressed her cheek. She giggled. He shuddered. Coleman tried not to think about the slithering sensation as he sipped his coffee.

*

Coleman drank four martinis and then thought about making dinner for Sandra. When the tentacle emerged from his left nostril, weaving back and forth, trying to open the refrigerator door, he grasped it with both hands.

He tugged. It resisted. He pulled and pulled and it stretched out long and thin. It hurt like nothing he had ever felt before as an amorphous sack squeezed out through his nose and plopped onto the kitchen table. It reformed into a translucent blob, pathetic and quivering. Coleman retched. He didn't feel drunk anymore.

He reached for the phone.

Julie picked up on the third ring.

"It's me," he said.

"What's wrong?" she said.

"I'm an empty old man," he said. "I'm going to die."

"You're not old," she said. "What are you talking about?"

"I love you."

She was silent a moment. "Why don't you come over?"

He grabbed his acrylic heart from the mantel and hauled his trembling body to the car. He managed it somehow, using his own hands and feet on the wheel and pedals, surprised that he still knew how, that he had the strength.

He tried to imagine what Sandra would do when she got home and found the creature quivering on the kitchen table. Maybe she would let it go free. Maybe she would lay down her head and mourn its death. He decided he didn't care.

Julie met him outside her apartment, squinting through the rain at him.

The rain dripped down his nose, under his collar.

"Look at me," Coleman said. "There's nothing left but a hollow body. I don't want to live anymore."

She put a hand on his arm. "What about your bookstore?" she said.

"It's an unrealistic dream," he said.

"Is that what Sandra told you?"

He lowered his head.

"I don't think it is unrealistic," she said.

He felt the edges of his inside wound tighten just a little, start to pull together. Maybe it would fill in. Maybe the creature had not taken all of him. He stood up a little straighter.

"You broke up with Giles," he said.

"He was a jerk."

"I could have told you that."

The rain pattered lightly on the leaves of the jasmine bush near the walk.

"I've missed the rain," he said.

"I've missed the old Coleman," she said. "That crazy guy who bought dusty old books and piled them all over his apartment."

"Did I really do that?" he said.

He felt tears on his cheeks. He thought about saving and saving until he could afford the first few months rent on a store, about finding those books he had treasured so much as a child. Maybe Julie would want to help him with the bookstore. It suddenly didn't seem so unrealistic anymore.

She took the acrylic heart from under his arm. "I wish

you could put it back in," she said.

He smiled at Julie, at the rain, at the city. "It will grow back," he said. And he knew it was true.

The Giving Heart

Faith is a Nanooka

Manda sat on the terrace just before dawn and wondered what decision the doctors had made about her. The sun was contemplating making another showing and the sky was that deep blue-gray that could go either way. Only the birds let on that it was the start of another day and not the end, with their complete faith in the sunrise, and that's what she figured another day was all about anyway: faith.

Her great nephew Tyler approached the residence gates, which scanned him and let him enter without breaking stride. She hadn't expected him to come by so early, and she felt resentful. She had wanted to be alone in the quiet of the morning, pretending the shush of electric trains was the ocean, pretending Tony was sitting beside her. Tony would have loved the roses in the gardens, the way they shed the night's condensation and opened up to the sun every day. He would have made fun of the fact that the place was called an Active Life Residence rather than a Senior Citizen Home, would have drunk tea with her in the mornings on the terrace, would have helped her understand the decision about the hospital.

"Good morning, Aunt Manda."

Tyler stood in front of her, snowflakes melting on his EnviroCoat. He switched off the field and the snow fell, disintegrating like dust before it reached the ground.

Nanooka burst from Manda's lap and begin circling Tyler's ankles, yapping.

He swatted at the dog with his briefcase. "Can't you program it to stop that?" he said.

"Come here, Nanooks," Manda said. The little dog hopped onto Manda's lap and sat panting. "Nanooka is fine the way he is," she said.

"*It* is a nuisance."

"*He* loves me."

"It's a machine," he said. "Just because it has fur and is programmed to—"

"Don't you dare," she said.

Tyler sighed. "What are you doing outside so early? You'll catch chill."

"Oh, please. They keep it sixty five degrees in the gardens all year. God knows what temperature it is out there."

"Twenty eight," he said. "Still."

She waited, watching him stand awkwardly, gripping his briefcase like it was a shield. He'd had a rough start of it, what with his father in and out of prison, but he had done all right despite all of that. He had helped her out after Tony died. But now her savings was gone and she had an illness that everyone talked around, something about an aneurism waiting to happen, which she gathered meant she wouldn't live that long, even if she went to the hospital.

Invite him in for a cup of tea, Tony would have said. God knew he was always the nicer of the two of them.

"Oh, for Pete's sake," she said.

"What's that?" Tyler said.

"Would you like a cup of tea?"

"Yes, that would be nice."

Inside, she set Nanooka down and reached in the cupboard for her electric kettle. Her shoulder stiffened at the sudden movement, refused to budge.

Tyler reached over her and lifted the kettle down. "I'll do it," he said. "You go sit down."

"Don't patronize me," she said.

He froze, clearly hurt.

He's just a kid. Tony's voice in her head. He means well. That was her Tony, always so goddamned good hearted.

"What?" Tyler said.

She tried to soften her tone. "Let me make the tea. It's the only thing I can do anymore."

He moved to the living room couch, only a few feet away

from the kitchenette. She filled the kettle and plugged it in—no open flame for the Active Life Residents.

He sat forward on the couch. "I spoke to the residence staff this morning," he said.

Here it comes, she thought.

"They want you to go to the hospital."

"But there's nothing they can do."

"They'll monitor you. The doctors are right there in case things get worse."

"I don't want to go to the hospital," she said. "Besides, I don't understand why I can't take Nanooks."

"It belongs to the residence."

"But he's imprinted on me now."

"They'll reprogram—"

"No," she said. It wasn't possible. Nanooks loved her, and no one else.

"Aunt Manda, we don't have a choice. I'm sorry. I'm really sorry. I know you love it—him."

He gave her a rueful smile, looked like he wanted to say more, then changed his mind.

The kettle saved her with its insistent burbling. She put two bags into ceramic cups, filled them with hot water. She took her time carrying the cups the short walk to the coffee table. She settled into her easy chair with Nanooks on her lap, her tea at her side. Perfect, she thought, except that it would all be gone soon.

It wasn't much of an apartment, really. It was identical to

all the others in the residence, with its kitchenette off the small living room, a window that could look out onto the hibiscus hedge or show a Costa Rican beach, three fake plants with leaves that changed color to indicate the season outside. And of course, Nanooka. He made it all worthwhile.

She hadn't expected that. The little creature had greeted her the first day with his tail wagging and little pink tongue hanging out of his mouth.

"A dog?" she had said, incredulous.

"Well, almost," her floor helper had answered. "The residents often enjoy them, but of course if you don't want—"

She had already knelt down slowly and painfully onto one knee, and held out her hand to Nanooka, who sniffed her fingers. "No," she said. "This will work out just fine."

Nanooka reminded her of Cooper, her first and only dog. Cooper had followed her home from the neighborhood park one weekend when she was eight years old, even jumping into the elevator with her, and she had kept Cooper a secret for exactly one night before her mother discovered him and took him away. Even after all these years, she still remembered Cooper's trusting eyes.

Tony had liked dogs but had been terribly allergic, and Manda had loved Tony enough to marry him and forego pets. In the years since Tony died, she hadn't thought about getting a dog. For one thing, she didn't have the energy to take care of anyone except herself. But mostly, she hadn't believed that her heart could ever bear loving another creature again.

She realized that Tyler had been speaking.

"I'm sorry," she said. "What did you say?"

"Tomorrow," he said.

"Tomorrow?" She felt disoriented, as if she had been dropped into someone else's conversation.

"Let me know if you need help packing. I can come back any time."

She held Nanooka tightly to her chest and he gave a soft whimper. He always knew when she was frightened or agitated.

"That's too soon," she said.

"I'm sorry, Aunt Manda. They were insistent." He paused, pursed his lips. "Have you thought about how you want, that is to say, whether you want—" He trailed off, a pained expression on his face.

"A funeral?" she said. "No, I haven't thought about that. Why does it matter? I won't be around for it."

The truth was she had thought about death and religion a lot in the past few days. She used to believe in God the way she believed the sun would rise every day, something she didn't question. But now that her Nanooka was going to be taken away, now that she would have nothing left, now that she knew the end of her life was much closer than the beginning, she had started to wonder about it all. It just didn't add up. That benevolent god had taken Tony away from her. That loving god was going to let her die alone in a hospital.

A sudden fierce anger rose inside her. "I don't believe in

god anymore," she said. "If he does exist, he's a jerk."

She was glad to hear her voice could still be strong, even when her joints and muscles betrayed her on a daily basis. Nanooka jumped out of her lap and barked, ran in a circle, then jumped back on her lap.

Tyler shook his head.

"What?" she said. "You think God will strike me down for saying that?"

"No," he said. "I don't think it matters what you say or believe. You can hate god, or think god is taking care of you, or not believe in god at all. But in the end it doesn't really matter."

"So what matters?"

"What matters is that we should all take care of each other the best we can." He smiled. "Even if someone has a Nanooka that keeps trying to bite your ankles."

There was a little of Tony in him, she thought. Why hadn't she ever seen that before? Her anger was gone, evaporated into thin air like the night's condensation gone to the sun.

*

Manda woke later in the afternoon and knew something was wrong. Tony was gone, yes, that was wrong and had been wrong for a while. But this was different. Her tiny apartment was too still. After a moment, she figured it out.

"Nanooka!" she said.

At her voice, the overheads flooded the bedroom. She blinked in the sudden brightness. Everything was in its place: from her bedroom door she could see the kitchenette and half the living room. The residence staff had been in to vacuum the carpet, to put the kettle up into the cupboard.

"Nanooks!"

She got herself vertical, ignoring the ache in her knees and hips, the throbbing of her shoulder. She searched the apartment. She put on her sweater, opened her back terrace door, and walked slowly through the garden.

"Nanooka!" Manda called. "Nanooks!"

The door to her adjoining apartment opened and Trisha appeared in the doorway, tying her bathrobe. "Lost your dog?"

Manda shuffled over.

Trisha was ninety, going on forty. Her skin shone from the creams she applied religiously. Her hair was auburn, with hints of blonde, shoulder length. Her teeth were a perfect even white. "Age is an illusion," she had said on more than one occasion. But her eyes gave her away, Manda thought. Too much experience.

"It's not a dog," Manda said, and found bitterness in her voice.

Trisha looked at Manda for a moment. "Did he run away?"

"No," Manda said. "The residence took him back."

"But why? He's imprinted on you."

"Because I have to go to the hospital." She couldn't help

it; her voice broke.

"I'm so sorry." Trisha reached out and took Manda's hand between her own. Her skin felt cool, her bones small and delicate like a bird. Brittle, Manda thought. That's what happened when you got old. Everything got fragile and then it disintegrated. Dust to dust.

She had to pull herself together.

"Are you religious?" Manda said, before she could stop herself. You're too impulsive, Tony always used to say. You can't just say everything that comes into your head. But now that she was old she could say whatever she wanted and no one batted an eye.

Trisha smiled. "I believe religion is like underwear. You know everyone is wearing some, but you aren't supposed to ask about it."

And that's what gave her age away, Manda thought. Trisha was clever and diplomatic.

"Maybe they sent your dog back to the factory," Trisha said.

To be reprogrammed. She didn't say it but Manda knew she was thinking it.

*

The moment she stepped from the residence gates, the air assaulted her face, her hands, and even that was not enough: the cold immediately began its slow creep down the back of her coat.

She had forgotten about the winds off the lake, the air like ice in her lungs. She pulled her purse in tight, wrapped her arms around her torso. She wished she had taken Tyler up on his offer to buy her an EnviroCoat.

A tiger leapt for her, giant paws outstretched, claws long and sharp.

She pulled back, her breath caught in her throat. But the cat swept clean through her and bounded on down the street.

"Sorry!" A young woman jogged by, waved with her holo control.

"How rude!" Manda said. But the woman was already lost in the throng of pedestrians. She could see flashes of orange and black as the tiger leapt along the sidewalk, right through everyone and everything. No one paid it any attention. A few others had holo pets: a monkey here, a parrot there, a few dogs. When people passed close to each other their EnviroCoat fields glittered where they intersected, looked almost like those old-fashioned snow globes that she had as a girl.

Except that everyone moved so fast, pushing past each other and in and out of shop fronts that spilled light and sound, flashing images too fast for her to make sense of, songs that sounded like nothing more than noise. Only a few others had regular coats like hers, collars turned up, heads down against the razor air.

An electric train blurred to a stop in the center of the street, disgorged people into the middlewalk. Cars and busses spilled around it, like water finding its way past a rock in the river. No wonder no one from the residence ever went outside, she thought.

She realized she was pressed against the residence gates. She steadied herself, pushed into the moving crowd, and was immediately jostled side to side. One man stumbled around her, gave her a dirty look.

She tried to focus on her mission. One step after another, one breath after another, and finally she was at the first shop. She stepped inside and rubbed her hands together, felt the tingling in her cheeks from the warm air.

"Are you lost?" a voice said.

She focused on a young man. He looked to be of Indian descent. How could he possibly hear with those buds in his ears?

"Where would you take a Nanooka to be reprogrammed?" she said.

"A Nanooka? I don't know. But there's a Mega just three blocks down. They sell Nanookas and they might know."

Three long blocks, with traffic lights that were too fast for an old woman.

"Want a ride?" he said.

"Are you planning on robbing me?" she said.

He frowned and pulled the buds from his ears. "Of course not."

"Because I don't have any money. And everything I own is managed by someone else."

"I just happen to be heading that way, is all."

He didn't look quite as young anymore. He had an earnest frown, like he was genuinely puzzled that she might think ill of him.

She agreed to the ride.

He had her wait outside the store while he went to retrieve his electric. He helped her in, got her safety belt adjusted, and then they drove for two minutes in a blur and whiz of cars before he pulled into a bus loading zone.

"It's right there," he said, pointing to a store entrance that looked for all the world like a giant mouth, lights like teeth around the edges.

"Can I ask you something?" She didn't wait for him to say yes. "Do you believe in god?"

"Listen, I don't mean to be rude, but I don't need a sermon." He glanced in the rear-view mirror. A bus was approaching.

"I'm just curious," she said. Because I'm going to die soon, she didn't say.

"I believe in lots of gods," he said. "I'm Hindu."

"Really? I don't mean to be rude, but you don't sound very convincing."

"Well, the way I see it, why not believe in god? I mean, it's a good story, right? I can believe or not believe, and believing gives my life meaning, so I might as well believe."

The bus honked, loud and strident.

"Can I help you get out?" he said.

"But you can't just make yourself believe in something," she said.

He was cute when he was anxious, she thought, all those lines creasing his face like a wrinkled napkin.

"Please, Ma'am, I'd like to stay and talk but—"

The bus honked again.

She opened the door and turned as she stood up slowly, making eye contact with the bus driver the entire time. The bus driver was a young woman who stared back, then threw up her hands and opened the bus door, letting her passengers out in the street instead of at the curb.

She could tell the young man was relieved to be on his way.

You shouldn't have pestered him, Tony would have said.

Tony, a part of her life for so many years, and then suddenly gone. Now that was something she still couldn't quite believe.

The store was overheated, the windows fogged with condensation, and her coat was starting to smell like a wet dog.

A saleswoman approached. "Can I help you find something?" She was middle-aged, with a glossy phone implant that matched her earrings. She stared above Manda's head and waited, stifling a yawn.

"I heard you sell Nanookas—"

"Right this way."

"No, actually—"

Manda caught up with the woman near a shelf of batteries that didn't look at all like the batteries of her youth, with their fancy green casings and nubs for bio-connects.

"The truth is that I've lost my Nanooka," she said to the saleswoman before she could march off again. "I mean, someone stole him. And I want him back. Where would they take him if they were going to reprogram him?"

"Well." The woman stroked her phone implant. "Probably back to the factory. They can reprogram the unit there, or you can get a trade-in, or sometimes cash."

"The factory?"

"You know, the one out on Nanoway. It's attached to the warehouse shopper."

"Are you religious?" Manda said.

The woman lowered her gaze, finally made eye contact. "No, actually. Why?"

"You have to admit it's tempting. You know, that someone all powerful is watching out for us. That we have souls that live on."

"Yes. I'd agree that it's tempting to believe. But I don't."

"Why not?"

"I don't know exactly. Maybe because it sounds too easy."

"Like your job," she said.

The woman smiled, and Manda saw that she was in fact a beautiful woman. She wondered if she enjoyed her life, despite the boredom of being a salesperson at a Mega.

"Sorry to pester you," she said.

"No problem. Really. You're the most interesting thing that's happened all day."

"How can I get to Nanoway?" she said.

"You have a car?"

"No."

"Then you'll have to take the train. Or the bus."

She opted for the bus, because it was slower.

*

She watched the trees pass by in regular intervals, wondering at how they managed through all the human contraptions of concrete and metal. There was apparently dirt down there somewhere.

The bus trundled down the main road and onto a smaller road and suddenly the traffic lightened like a switch thrown. There were houses that looked like houses, packed up against each other, but with a pleasant absence of flashing lights and dancing holos.

Someone sat heavily in the seat next to her.

"Beautiful, isn't it?"

He was wiry, with long tangled throw-back hair and pale orange robes.

"Krishna?" she said.

"Gnostic," he said, his face beaming. "One people, one god. We're all the same and god lives in each and every one of us. You just have to feel the love."

"It is a good story," she said.

His face changed abruptly. "It's not a story."

"I meant that it's a nice way—"

"It's the truth!"

"All right, then."

"You don't understand!"

She pressed herself against the window to avoid his hand which was clenching into a fist in the air in front of her.

She touched her cheekbone. "I'm calling the police now."

He glared at her, then stood up and moved away, muttering to himself. "Truth," she heard. "Beauty."

She waited until he was hunched into a seat at the back, then moved to sit right behind the bus driver for the rest of the ride.

The bus dropped her in a snow-dusted valley between twin mountains of parking structures and warehouses. The snow was coming down as sparse fluff, lightly coating car roofs and the EnviroCoats of people funneling in to the main warehouse entrance. Her breath spilled white into the air in front of her until she crossed the entrance field.

She wandered up aisles of gigantic boxes of crackers and cookies, containers of peanut butter that would take her a year to get through, flats of every imaginable soda. She came to a long shelf of dolls and Nanookas, perfectly clean and groomed within their plastic boxes, eyes open but unseeing. The boxes were covered in complex instructions in small writing that she could barely read. But none of these were her Nanooka, her little companion who knew her and barked at Tyler and nuzzled her cheek whenever she thought about Tony.

She approached an older gentleman in an orange vest who was placing boxes onto the shelves.

"How do I get to the factory?" she said. She looked at his nametag. "Henry."

"It's that way," he said, gesturing toward the back of the store. "But you aren't allowed in there."

"What about the recycle center? For Nanookas and other pets?"

"Is yours broken?"

"No. He was stolen."

"Oh. I'm sorry. You're better off going to animal control. They can locate by chip number—"

"Never mind." She turned away.

"Hey," he said. "I'll take you to the recycle center."

He hobbled past her, favoring one leg. Just like Tony, she thought, in those later years with his bum knee. But that had never stopped him. He had hobbled off of busses to see the Grand Canyon with her, hobbled onto airplanes and down trails. Hobbled around the apartment while fiddling with his collection of electric motors.

Electric is the future, he used to say. It'll save the world. Tony had believed in humanity. He looked at the arc of civilization and saw an upward trend. He believed people would ultimately not destroy their world and that maybe someday they would even reach the stars. His tireless optimism had buoyed him up in life and floated him through every hardship, every setback. Whatever had he seen in her, with her tireless cynicism and deep suspicion of people?

"Don't cry, M'lady. I'll give you a ride in my chariot."

Henry was back, driving an electric go-car with a stack of cardboard boxes on the back.

She wiped her eyes and climbed into the go-car, sitting on one of the boxes.

"This is probably not allowed," she said.

"Damn right," he said. "What's your name, my accomplice in crime?"

"Manda."

"Okay, Manda. Petal to the metal."

The go-car whirred past shelves at a rate only slightly faster than she would have been able to walk.

"Hang on!" Henry said.

They sped around a corner, but were overtaken by a toddler and had to screech to a stop. A woman swept by, scooping up the toddler with practiced ease.

"Kids these days," Henry muttered. She wasn't sure if he was talking about the toddler or the woman.

They continued on, moving past throngs of people pushing gigantic carts loaded with supplies as if they were preparing for an alien invasion. She tried to imagine stocking up for an alien invasion, deciding what items she might want. Tea, definitely. Maybe some wine, in case she needed to barter. She tried to imagine sitting at home with her Nanooks, listening to the news of the aliens breaching the outskirts of the city, then marching down to the city center, taking control of Megastores and electric trains, finally the Active Life Residences. It might be a welcome relief, she thought, to throw in the towel, say goodbye to it all.

"What was that?" Henry said.

"How far to the recycle center?"

"Two parsecs," he said.

She wasn't sure what he meant, but it sounded official. "Are you going to get in trouble?" she said.

"Probably not," he said. "The managers mostly leave me alone because I'm old. I just pretend to be confused if I do something wrong."

They swung toward a sliding door that opened when the go-car approached. Inside were more stacks of boxes, all the way to the high ceiling.

"Wow," she said.

"Yes," he said. "Like a cathedral. The religion of food."

She laughed, in spite of herself, in spite of having lost her Nanooka and being in a strange place with a stranger on a journey she hadn't anticipated.

"I've met a lot of interesting people today," she said. "I pestered all of them."

They passed bins of apples, more than she would eat in a year. The air was getting colder.

She was speaking before she knew she would. "Everyone had a different take on god, on religion. I met a Hindu, an atheist, and a crazy Gnostic."

"Were you pestering them or were they pestering you?" Henry said.

The warehouse doors ended in a wide loading dock and three electric conveyer belts.

"Religion is too pat," she said. "Obviously made up by people who want meaning in their lives."

"It's still a mystery," he said. "Life is a mysterious gift. Sudden and brief."

They sped down a ramp and into the bright winter air.

Light reflected down from thick white clouds. Further ahead another giant door was open to the elements, trucks lined up on either side. The snow was falling thicker now, the flakes forming a private tunnel just for them.

You can believe whatever you want, she thought. Maybe that was part of the gift—making your own meaning. The snowflakes stuck to her coat, her boots. It didn't feel as cold as it had before.

Henry raised a hand in greeting to two men in factory orange who stood in the doorway. They raised coffee cups in reply, gave Manda puzzled looks as the car whirred past.

"You should have been a spy," Manda said.

"How do you know I wasn't?"

They passed lines of large bins. Machinery pulled pieces from the bins, sorted them into smaller bins. After a moment she recognized the pieces: Legs and fur coats and heads. Synthetic eyes with wiring still attached.

Further in were the intact Nanookas, lines and lines of them on tables that went on forever. Curly fur coats covered small torsos and legs. Suspended robotic arms fed chips into waiting heads of circuitry.

That was all it was, she thought. Plastics and metals.

But no, that wasn't all. What were people besides dense bags of protein and water, phosphates and carbon, bones and minerals and salts? And rising out of that gelatin of chemicals was love. Love: tangible and profound. Love had been an anchor in her life, a thing more real than the air she breathed. She had loved Tony more than anything else, and he had loved her, and that had been bigger than either of them. Love had given her life meaning. So why couldn't there be love from a mechanical thing, a constructed thing, a metal and synthetic fur thing that whimpered and barked and knew when she was sad?

"Manda?" Henry said.

She had somehow slipped from the go-car and was lying on the floor, looking up into the rafters of robotic arms. She could just see the pink Nanooka noses over the lip of the closest table.

Henry's face was longer now, his features changing into someone familiar.

"Tony," she said. "Is that really you?"

He took her hand. "I've called the medics," he said.

"Don't be sad," she said. "I'm okay. I really am."

At the sound of her voice, one of the Nanookas jumped

from the table and ran to her, wagging his tail, his nose wet on her face.

"Look, Tony," she said. "I've found our Nanooka."

She tried to raise an arm to pet him, but her limbs wouldn't obey her. Nanooka put his head against hers and breathed in her ear. This was love, she thought. She really believed it.

And so it was true.

The Sound of Science

"And from here you can see the true size of the synchrotron," I say, pointing along the arc of the experimental hall. This part of the tour never fails to impress people, and I'm always a bit awed myself. "The x-rays that come off that ring are a billion times brighter than the sun and we use them to—"

"Excuse me."

I look at my tour group to see who has spoken, and find the Slug staring back at me with its three sets of protruding eyes. The rest of the tour, a middle school class from Oxford, is standing a discreet few feet away, which isn't surprising. The aliens have a peculiar odor; petrol and over-cooked fish are the kindest descriptions I've heard. Plus, they leave a trail of mucus wherever they go.

The term 'Slug' isn't the nicest name for our alien visitors, but it fits. The alien's lumpy, mucus-coated body sits in unpleasant contrast to the clean lines of the experimental hall. It stands on a Segway, and two tentacles grasp the handles in a parody of human hands. A viscous puddle has formed on the footstand.

"Do you study nucleic acid?" it says, its voice coming from somewhere under the eyestalks. "Here at Diamond Light Source?"

"Yes, we do. We have several structural biology beamlines, where we use x-ray diffraction to get the atomic structure of both proteins and nucleic acids—"

"What about three-strand DNA?"

I try to suppress my irritation. I'm doing this tour as a favour to a colleague, who is away at a conference. I should really be preparing for my own conference, plus I've got two papers that need editing and a fast-approaching grant deadline. Certainly the aliens already know everything they need to know about their three-stranded DNA.

"We haven't used these beamlines to study three-stranded DNA or its associated proteins," I say. "Your proteins are difficult to isolate and impossible to grow up in our usual cell lines. But surely you know that."

"Triple is best," the alien says. "Far superior to double DNA. Triple interactions and a hundred times the amino acids."

"A hundred more things that can go wrong," I say. "A hundred times the difficulty in replication and expression and repair of DNA."

The Slug ignores me and goes on about the superiority of three-stranded DNA. I try to arrange my face in a semblance of patience. They are to be treated as honored guests, after all. But it's hard to imagine that the synchrotron offers any technology they haven't already developed themselves, with their light-speed ships and translator nanobots that allow them to talk in any human language. Why they are visiting earth at all is a mystery to me. Yet here they are, touring castles and historic villages, museums and zoos. And synchrotrons.

Finally, the alien winds down. The cilia on its torso twitch, and its eyestalks undulate restlessly.

I want to argue. I want to ask why they feel the need to come here and tell us they are better than us. But instead, I go on with the tour. "All these beamlines are housed in the same building." I lift a hand to indicate the huge span of the hall, the circular wall that goes off into the distance. "And this makes for great acoustics. Let's just stop and listen for a moment."

From where we stand, we can hear the hum of computers, the swish and click of pumps and electronics, and underneath it all, the rise and fall of conversations from the scientists and engineers who work the floor. "Hear that?" I say. "It's the sound of discovery." This always gets them.

"You have all these techniques," the alien voice grates from behind me. "Why are you not studying triple DNA?"

I turn. I know I should do my best and just answer the question. I really do know that.

"We are not studying triple DNA here. I am not studying it because I do not have grant money to study it. And you know why? Because it would take years to figure out how to make our cell lines incorporate your superior triple DNA and produce your superior proteins. And years to figure out how to crystallize it. And I don't see any of you arrogant triple DNA slugs offering to help!"

I realize suddenly that everyone is staring at me. Two middle-schoolers who were previously fighting over a notebook have stopped to gape at my outburst. The adult chaperones look disapproving.

The alien doesn't respond, and if three pairs of eyes on stalks can manage to look hurt, somehow they do.

I represent science, I remind myself. I represent all scientists here at this facility.

"Ah, sorry," I say. "Let's move on, shall we?"

The alien is quiet after that. It tags along behind the rest of the tour. I feel reproach in the whir of the Segway wheels against the polished floor. I almost wish it would start talking about its DNA again.

*

Three days later I am sitting in the atrium enjoying a moment of quiet and a cup of coffee when I suddenly smell petrol.

I look up to see an alien approaching me on a Segway. They all look alike to me, but I have a feeling this is the same one that was on my tour. It confirms my suspicion when it says, "I understand that slugs are considered disgusting by your people."

"It was unkind to call you a slug," I say. "I'm sorry."

Its eyestalks make circular patterns in the air, a sign of embarrassment. I know that now because I've been doing some reading about the aliens.

It's a beautiful day, with sunlight streaming through the high windows to light the atrium in soft whites. The alien's skin gleams wetly in the light. I wonder if it hates the dry air here.

"I enjoyed your tour," it says.

"Thank you."

"I understand I interrupt too much."

"That's okay."

I sip my coffee, wondering how I can get out of the conversation. The grant application awaits. And one of the beamlines is down because of a problem with an ion pump. I have to reschedule a whole week of users.

"I'm curious," I say. "Why have you traveled all those light years to see the museums of earth? How could they possibly be that interesting to you?"

"What we have not seen is interesting. What we have seen seems ordinary."

"Very profound." I immediately regret my sarcasm, but to

my surprise the alien wiggles the fringes of cilia circling its eyestalks: its own form of laughter.

In spite of myself, I smile.

"And to reach for knowledge outside oneself—that is extraordinary."

That's something my father would have said. He was always reading about new technology and new science. He loved tours. He would have loved to meet the aliens. He would have followed them around, peppering them with questions.

I wait, but the alien doesn't say more. Perhaps it is feeling awkward. Maybe it doesn't know what to say to me, either.

"Listen," I say. "I'm heading down to troubleshoot one of the beamlines. Do you want to come along?"

"Yes, please."

I walk next to the alien, the wheels of its Segway squeaking a little, and I badge us through onto the experimental floor. I've been studying pictures of our visitors, and I think I can now distinguish some of the machines it carries. The recording devices are slight bumps under its skin, embedded at regular intervals along its torso. Its breathing apparatus is a series of translucent veils that cover its skin in patches, fluttering up as we move along. I know they wear a thin film of material to keep their skin moist. Maybe on their home world they don't leak mucus all the time.

"How do you travel on your home world?" I say. "Surely you don't have Segways?"

"Where we live is much like one of your swamps. We

half-swim, I think you would say."

We stop at the broken beamline, and I lead the alien back along the beampipe to a cluster of pumps and racks of electronics. It has to abandon its Segway along the way, and I try not to look at the trail its footpad leaves on the floor. I'll have to apologize to the cleaning staff later.

Now that I'm here, I'm wishing I hadn't invited the alien down. I'll tell it a little more about the beamline, then try to politely suggest it go tour something else. Maybe I can palm it off on one of my colleagues in the molecular biology lab.

"Here," the alien says. It extends a gray tentacle to one of the bellows connecting one section of pipe to an optics tank.

"Here what?" I say.

"A small leak. I plug it." It retrieves its arm back into its torso. A glistening pellet covers the place on the bellows that it touched. I look at the ion gauge, see that the pressure has started to drop. So the pump wasn't broken after all.

"How did you know there was a leak there?" I say.

"We have very sensitive recording equipment. We record not just sight and sound, but pressure and smell and other characteristics of the environment."

"But how does it work?"

"I cannot say," it says.

"Of course."

Maybe I haven't kept the disappointment out of my voice, because its eye stalks start to wave, and it says, "I do not mean to be disrespectful. Let me ask. Do you have an automobile?"

"Yes."

"Do you understand its operation?"

"Well, basically. It uses gasoline to fire pistons, which then, er, well, turn something, a crank of some sort…in the engine." I stare back at the alien for a moment. "I see your point."

"I am not the inventor of these sensing devices, or of the ships we travel in."

"Okay. But surely some of you understand the technology."

"It was given to us."

"Was it another race that gave you the technology?" I say. I imagine a universe filled with omniscient alien races, the vast knowledge they must possess. Maybe they've even unraveled the secrets of the birth of the universe itself—

"No," the alien says.

"No?"

"My people invented the ships, and the rest of our technology. But only some know how to build and maintain and fix."

"Only some of you, as in, not any of you that have come here?" I think I'm beginning to understand what the aliens are doing here.

"We wanted to travel, to see the universe. Like you travel in a car. We travel in a ship."

I study the alien for a moment, wondering exactly how much recording equipment it wears. "You're tourists," I say.

"Yes. We contribute for many years for the betterment of our race. Now we are free to travel and explore."

"You're *retired* tourists."

"Yes."

"That explains a lot," I say.

"Many wish to see what they haven't seen before. And many hope to find cures for all that kills us."

"Well, many of us hope that, too. That's what the work here is all about."

"No, you don't understand. We are retired because we are sick."

I study the alien some more.

"Only the sick are free to travel," it says.

"So sick that you can't work?"

"So sick that we will die soon, and we would like to spend the last of our days touring."

"But you must have ways to study your physiology. You must have the equivalent of synchrotrons on your home planet, and medicines and technology—" I trail off. To someone who lived a hundred years ago on earth, the technology today would seem miraculous. Yet we still have not cured cancer, or a myriad of other diseases.

"A hundred times the things that can go wrong," the alien says. Its eyes move up and down, a smile. "As you say."

They are advanced in metallurgy and mechanics. Not advanced enough in the biology of themselves. Not unlike us.

"All creatures die," I say.

"Just so."

Its breathing veils move up and down in the air currents, and every now and then tiny rainbows shimmer to life on the surfaces. I hadn't noticed that before.

My father died of lung cancer just five years ago, right before the aliens arrived. I would love to find a cure for cancer, too.

I start to think about ways that we could grow up cells that would incorporate triple-stranded DNA. It would take a lot of work. There are no preliminary experiments to put into the grant application. Yet their physiological building blocks are amino acids and nucleic acids. They harness oxygen for energy. They have cells and organs and circulatory systems and eyeballs. In some ways, they really aren't so different from us.

I stand there with the alien, listening to the rhythmic clang of pumps, the hiss of pneumatics and the whir of motors.

"Maybe I can look into that triple DNA system of yours," I say.

It's too late for these aliens, the current visitors. But we could help the ones that come next. And studying their nucleic makeup would certainly tell us something about our own. Maybe reaching outside ourselves is exactly what we need to do. Maybe that is the extraordinary that science is all about.

All Things are Full of Gods

May 2

We flew into Lhasa today. Mom was sick from the altitude, but Dad and I were fine. He says his lungs and blood remember even after all these years, and I'm half him and that's why I'm okay. Never mind that I grew up in Fort Collins, Denver. Mom said that was silly but she didn't laugh. I remember when she used to laugh at all his silly jokes.

The birds here seem upset. In the taxi from the airport I saw lots of bright-colored little flags and some chickens and lots of ravens. One of the ravens tried to tell me something but Mom was watching me so I ignored him.

I've started pretending I can't understand them when

Mom is around. She thinks there is something wrong with me. Before we left for Tibet I heard her telling Dad they should send me to a special school for girls like me. He said no way. She said it would make me better but Dad said there is nothing wrong with me. I'm afraid to tell Dad I can talk to birds because maybe he'll think I'm crazy too and then I won't have anyone who believes in me.

I think I'm the reason Mom and Dad argue all the time now. Maybe that's also why we came to Tibet. That, and the Atishans and the meteor.

I saw Atishans from the taxi, too. They were wearing their white robes and carrying signs about the meteor. They didn't look crazy like they do on the news at home.

Now we're at the hotel. Dad got called right away to go help at the UN and Mom is lying in bed with a washcloth on her forehead so I'm on my own.

I think I'll sneak out so I can find out why the raven was upset.

May 3

Dad didn't get back until really late last night. Mom was asleep. I was going to tell him what the ravens told me, but then he pulled something from his pocket that was small and round and brownish and he told me exactly the same thing the ravens said! He said the little balls fell from the meteor, thousands of them all over the north part of the city and in the forest and all the way to the desert where the meteor crashed.

Dad said no one knew what they were. I said maybe they were eggs, like I was making a guess even though I knew for sure because that's what the ravens said, and birds are usually right about things like that. He said some scientists thought they might be eggs, but everyone else said the scientists were wrong. I wanted to ask if the scientists talked to the birds here, but I didn't. But maybe there are other people like me and maybe I'm not crazy. I wish I could ask Dad.

He put the egg away and said we get to go on a tour of the meteor tomorrow, if Mom is feeling up to it.

May 4

I'm so upset I can barely write. When Mom woke up this morning she asked me about talking to the ravens and I said no that was silly. But then she asked, do they sound like people? And I thought she really wanted to know so I started to tell her about how they don't talk in words, it's more like little bits of thought that kind of piece together like a jigsaw puzzle and make sense inside my head. And then she said, do the ravens here sound like the ravens at home? I said yes, and then she looked at me like that proved something. She said enough is enough and if I persisted in pretending that I could talk to animals that I would not be allowed to go see the meteor.

I started to cry and I said this is the way I am, I can't help it, and she said I could stay in this stupid hotel room until I came around. She and Dad went out for a while. Then Dad came back to talk to me. He said he would let me go on the tour, but I had to tell Mom that I would stop talking to birds. I asked if he believed me and he said maybe but most people wouldn't understand and it would make my life easier if I just pretended I couldn't. I said like he pretended to love Mom? Then he looked really hurt and I said I was sorry.

May 5

The stupid tour got delayed anyway. All these Atishans filled up the road with a protest and then a bunch of Chinese soldiers came and tried to get them to move and there were some fights. The UN decided we should just wait until everyone calmed down.

We stayed in the hotel most of the day and Mom wouldn't let me out of her sight except to go to the bathroom. Dad didn't even go to the UN. He told me stories about the gods of Tibet.

Dad said the Atishans believe that the meteor is their god Manjursi. They think that sometimes their gods come down from Heaven and then get stuck here and can't go back. They think another god fell a thousand years ago and his name is Tillet.

I said their gods must be kind of weak. He just smiled and said it's not possible to know what the gods think or why they do what they do. Mom said there is only one god, and then Dad said it can't hurt to learn a little mythology, and Mom said the Atishans are crazy and then they started arguing about Tibet so I went back to my room and turned my ipod up high. The news here shows the same boring photos over and over: the meteor crashing and the Atishans blocking the roads, and the Chinese soldiers guarding the meteor and all the UN people and the scientists from all over the world who want to come and study the meteor.

May 6

The most amazing thing happened. The meteor is a bird and I can talk to her!

What happened was we finally got to go on a tour of the meteor, which obviously isn't a meteor if you know anything at all.

First off, it didn't crash. It skidded across the ground for miles and miles. I saw the big black streak all the way across the desert from the truck on the way in. The road was filled with Atishans, but the area around the meteor was all fenced off. I think it's unfair that I can go see the meteor but the Atishans can't. It's their country.

Secondly, it definitely was not a rock. From the outside it maybe looks like a rock, red and brown and shiny. But it has tunnels. We went inside one. At first it was just like a cave, but then the walls turned squishy so we stopped and had to listen to the Chinese ambassador talk for a long time about all the countries working together to understand the meteor.

While he was talking something really strange happened. I leaned against one of the squishy walls and I had my hands behind me and they started to sink into the wall a little. I didn't say anything because then I heard her talking to me. Manjursi has traveled a really long way and she's looking for her mate. She held my hand in a friendly way while she showed me how she swims in the universe like it's a big ocean of stars.

But she got injured before she found her mate. She said something came from the ground and knocked her down and I think it was missiles. So now she's injured and she can't move.

Manjursi said she is really happy that I can hear her. I feel like I finally have a friend who understands me.

May 7

Mom and Dad had a big argument last night when they thought I was asleep. Mom wants to put me in a school for crazy kids when we get back. Dad said no. But I know he will lose if they get a divorce and she tells the judge that I talk to birds.

I want to tell Dad that Manjursi spoke to me but he might think I'm crazy, too.

I snuck outside when they were asleep and I found an Atishan woman in the all-night grocery. I asked if I could talk to her and she said yes so I told her that I could understand birds and that Manjursi spoke to me.

At first she looked like she didn't believe me and then she did. She took me to a big stone house that looked like a library and there was another Atishan woman there who was really old. She was covered in wrinkles but she was really nice. She talked to me for a long time and then she showed me a map of Tibet. She said one of the Atishans a really long time ago could also understand animals and that it was also a girl. The girl talked to Tillet. Tillet is waiting underground north of here. I saw on the map where he is waiting. He's been waiting more than a thousand years for Manjursi to bring him an egg.

I said why don't you just get an egg from the forest and bring it to Tillet? She said because all those eggs are dead. They can't survive if they get cold so they need to get an egg directly from Manjursi. But no one will let them get close to Manjursi and anyway everyone thinks they are crazy. I said I knew what that was like because my Mom thinks I am crazy and maybe my Dad, too, and then I couldn't help it I started crying. The old Atishan woman gave me a big hug and said Mom and Dad will believe me someday and it made me feel better even though I don't know if what she said was true.

May 9

I didn't write all day yesterday because Mom and Dad dragged me all over the city and when we got back I was so tired I went right to bed. Dad wanted to show me all the places he used to live and some old temples. They're acting all cheerful and friendly with each other and now I know for sure they are getting a divorce. I'm pretty sure the plan is for Dad to stay in Lhasa and for me to go back home with Mom. No way am I going with her.

Yesterday the birds followed me all over the temples and the roads and it made Mom really angry. There were ravens and little black birds with red on their tails and these pretty golden birds that looked like little flames when they fly. Dad said they were rose finches. Finally Mom got back in the taxi by herself and I had a chance to talk to Dad alone.

I told Dad I really needed to go back and tour the meteor again and he asked me why. I said because it was my destiny to help the Atishans and it was really unfair that nobody was letting them see their god. He said the world is not fair and that learning that is one of the hardest things about growing up. I said in that case maybe my destiny was to never grow up.

He didn't say anything for a little while and then he looked like he was going to cry and he said he would love me and be proud of me no matter what my destiny was.

I asked would he love me even if I could talk to birds, and he said yes. I asked if he would love me if I really couldn't talk to birds but I was crazy so I thought I could, and he said yes.

I almost changed my mind right then. But then I thought about Manjursi searching for thousands of years and Tillet waiting for thousands of years and I decided I have to go ahead with my plan.

May 10

Dad arranged for another tour. He knows I'm up to something but he hasn't asked me what. He said something funny tonight. He said "all things are full of gods". He said it is from an old Greek philosopher and it is his favorite quote of all time.

He looked at me like he is proud of me and he believes in me. I wish Mom would look at me like that.

I can't write anymore because it's really late and I have to get ready. I'm packing some sandwiches and water and a flashlight and the map the Atishan woman gave me and my diary. I have to be really careful that Mom and Dad don't wake up and see me packing.

May 11

So much has happened I can barely believe it.

I'm writing this from a tiny cave in the ground. It's really cold and my flashlight will probably run out soon but I have to write down what happened in case I don't come back.

What I did was I ran away on the tour. I mean I ran into Manjursi. I ran down the tunnel and I pushed myself against a wall and Manjursi surrounded me like a huge hug, only it was squishy walls all around me. Everyone was looking for me but they couldn't find me because I was hidden inside Manjursi.

Then Manjursi put an egg in my hand.

At first I was scared, but then Manjursi started talking to me and I can't even describe how amazing it was. It would take pages and pages and still no one would understand. Dad said everything is filled with gods and now I understand. I saw stars and other planets and other meteors like Manjursi and all the amazing things that live in the universe and I felt like I was all those things, all at once. Then Manjursi stopped talking and I was just me again.

But after that I wasn't angry at Mom anymore. I understand that she can't understand me and it scares her. I know she and Dad are probably really sad and scared right now and I feel bad about that. But I have to do this. I know for sure that I'm not crazy and I feel like I was born to help Manjursi and Tillet and it feels so right.

At first I was going to give the egg to the Atishans, but then I realized I couldn't get all the way back to Lhasa because it's too far. So instead I told Manjursi to let me out away from all the guards and people. She let me out when it was dark and there was no one around and I ran through the desert and found this cave.

The egg is a really pretty golden color. Whenever I let it sit out in the air too long it starts to get a little brownish, so I have to keep it close to my skin to keep it warm. I'm afraid to go to sleep because I might let it roll away and get cold.

I have to stop writing now because I need to go and try to find Tillet.

May 12 or 13

I think this is going to be the last time I write. I found Tillet. He is underground and I had to follow this small crack in the ground until it widened just large enough to let me in. I had to crawl on my hands and knees a really long way down. It took all night and then I think another day. I ate all my sandwiches and drank all my water already. But at least it is warm underground here with Tillet. He started talking and I almost cried when he showed me how much he loves Manjursi. He took the egg and the baby is growing inside him, just like a seahorse, because with seahorses the males carry the babies. Tillet is a starhorse.

I'm not hungry or lonely when Tillet talks to me. He's going to live long enough to make sure the baby is strong enough to fly fast off the earth before anyone can shoot her down. Maybe if she comes back in a thousand years we'll be ready to talk to her then and people will believe that some people can talk to animals and everyone will believe the amazing things that Manjursi and Tillet can show us.

Mom, if you're reading this I'm sorry I said mean things about you. I know you only want me to be happy and you didn't believe that I could hear animals so you thought it would make me unhappy because other people would think I was crazy. But if you ever read this I want you to know that I am happy now. I am happier than I have ever been because I know I did the right thing and I found my destiny and fulfilled it.

I'm going to sit inside Tillet now and listen to him while I go to sleep.

This Side of Kinsey

Sandy takes in my khakis, my boots, my crew cut.

"Oh," she says, "You must be the lesbian."

I smile. "I'm Jules Morgan. Tidy Token Agency."

She ushers me into the voluminous vestibule of her summer "cottage", motions toward the living room with a flutter of her hand, and then forgets about me as someone else arrives.

I hear her squeal-hellos fade as I head down the indicated hallway. I snag a plate of prosciutto from a passing tuxedo-clad waiter and station myself near the champagne.

A man in a deep skier tan and the latest in velvet slacks approaches.

"Make a lot of money doing this?" he says.

I shrug. "Enough." I'm not paid to be friendly.

"I've heard they hire straight Tokens at some parties in New York."

"Not here in Tidy."

"Maybe I could hire myself out," he says with a wink.

"The agency uses a battery of physiological response and pheromone tests to certify their people," I say.

He gives me a blank look.

"They don't make mistakes," I say.

He loses interest and goes off to talk to his skier buddies.

The party is boring, but I do my time. I watch the crowd, all rich and old and not-quite fashionable, all wishing they were young and hip. Tokens at their parties help them believe they're young and hip.

Trina arrives in the midst of the fashionably late crowd. She stands out with her blue-black skin against the red silk of her blouse, but she would stand out even if she weren't the only non-melanin-challenged person in the room. She's tall, with a long regal face, spiky dreads and eyes you could drown in.

She appeared in town just a few months ago. Usually she drags along some hulk of a guy, pinheads on large sloping shoulders. But tonight she's alone, and she looks uncomfortable. Which is strange, because normally she makes conversation with anybody, makes black look comfortable among white, which is, after all, what she's paid for.

At the end of the party, Sandy hands me the cash card

and says, "Are you available next Saturday? It'll be a much bigger party. Very high-end." She nods meaningfully at my khakis. I get the hint. I'll have to dress up. Maybe I'll splurge on some black slacks. But you bet I'll be there. Bigger party, bigger pay.

*

Next Saturday, Sandy doesn't call. It's not that I need the money so badly, but something about it bothers me, so I bend the agency rules just a little and call her.

"Oh, Jules," she says. "Sure I remember you. Sorry. I found another one."

"Another lesbian?" I say.

"Black and gay. Two birds. One stone. You know."

I fume but I end the conversation politely, and then I go through my mental list. Who could it be?

I call the three other lesbians in town, but they haven't heard of any newcomer. I do learn, however, that Cat is now sleeping with Gina, and Freda is threatening to leave town. The usual drama.

I call my agent, but she won't give me any information.

"I'm sorry, Jules," she says, staring out from my phone with a look of sympathy. "You know I can't talk about the other Tokens." She speaks in a soothing voice, as if I am angry. Which I am.

Either this new Token is from another area, encroaching on my party territory, or she's a fake, somehow duped the certification tests. Either way, I'm going to find out.

*

I wait on the walk in front of Sandy's mansion, pretending to talk into my cell. Limos pull up the manicured gravel driveway and disgorge women in elegant black dresses, men in tailored suits. One woman in baggy pants strolls up the driveway in flats. I look again.

Trina.

"No way," I say.

She sees me, stops. She's wearing cargo pants with a million pockets, no-nonsense Chelsea boots, and an oversized sweater.

"Kind of playing it up a bit, aren't you?" I say.

She looks away. "Just doing my job."

"My job! This was my job!"

"Sorry."

She shrugs, and for a moment she really does look comfortable in those clothes. She's even starting to slouch a little. And then I figure it out. It's under-the-counter 'mones. Has to be.

True orientation changing is still in the research stage, but for a small fee you can go to a black-market 'mones dealer, get a hormone cocktail injected directly into your pituitary, and for a day or two you'll be gay. Or straight. Or wherever on the Kinsey scale you want to sit. It's not exactly safe. There are a few cases of people going loopy and more than a few nasty infections from unclean needles.

But even that wouldn't fool the certification tests. How did she do it? I don't know much about 'mones, but I am determined to out her.

I stalk home, find my digital cam, buy an instant upload link with time and date and reality stamp certification. And then I wait, loitering in front of the row of high-end restaurants and cocktail lounges that make up most of downtown Tidy.

*

It's three days before I see her again, but when I do, I know I have her. She's with a big goon of a man, all neck and shoulders. I follow them into a retro disco establishment, glittery disco ball and high-pitched Bee-Gees, and everything served in gigantic martini glasses. I stand in the shadows behind the bouncer.

I'm ready to get a shot of her smooching with this hulk and send it in to the agency. She will be disqualified and I will get my job back. Take that, you wanna-be!

But something isn't right.

He has a meaty hand on her back, but she's not leaning in to him. In fact, she's ogling the women on the dance floor. And then every minute or so she shakes her head, as if she can't believe what she's doing. And then she starts staring again.

I have my camera ready, but there isn't one decent shot of

her and the goon. They're not smooching. They're not even holding hands.

Suddenly he leans over, yells something into her ear, then heads for the door. She follows, and I trail along behind.

I get outside in time to see him stalking away. She hugs herself, looking so sad I just can't help it. I go over.

"What are you doing here?" she says.

"Clubbing. Same as you."

"The gay bar is on the other side of town."

"I could say the same to you."

We glare at each other.

Finally, she relents. She puts her face in her hands and says something I can't understand. I guide her away from the clot of heteros hanging outside the club.

We're standing under an awning just south of main, and the winter air is chilly. She's shivering in her miniskirt, and she pulls at the spaghetti strings on her blouse as if they are bothering her.

"I don't know what's happening to me," she says.

"What exactly is happening to you?" I say.

She shakes her head. "I keep finding myself wanting to buy sensible shoes. Sleeping in instead of getting up early to do my hair and face—"

"You went to a 'mones dealer, didn't you?"

"Yesterday I woke up and put on those cargo pants without even realizing what I was doing. They just seemed so, I don't know, so practical. All those pockets." Her voice breaks.

"It's okay," I say. "It'll go away."

But I can't help my vindictive side from thinking: maybe she'll think twice about stealing my job again.

"I just don't want to end up with a mullet and those awful clothes—"

All right, I've had enough.

"You know," I say. "Some lesbians like those kinds of clothes."

"If I'm going to be a lesbian, I want to be a lipstick lesbian!"

"Well, put on some lipstick then!" Now I'm feeling defensive about my sneakers and jean jacket. "Butch and femme is so last century. You can be whatever you want."

"No, I can't! You don't understand."

She's right, I don't understand. "I'm going home," I say. I'm tired of this drama. This is exactly why I do not hang out with Freda and Cat and Gina.

"Don't go," she says softly.

She sinks down onto a planter box, squishing a row of marigolds, and starts to sob. I sit next to her, wondering what to do. I can't just leave her like this.

She wipes her eyes. Then I realize she has her hand on my knee. She gives my leg a squeeze.

"You don't want to do this," I say.

"Yes, I do."

"You're going to regret this when the 'mones wear off."

"Does that mean you're saying yes?"

*

The next morning I say, "We can go to parties as a couple and split the pay. Just until you revert."

She's just waking up, blinking sleepily in the early morning light. I've got the blinds programmed to open gradually, ease the morning in. I like the way she looks in the morning, slightly confused but happy, all the worries of the night a distant thing.

"I don't think I'm ever going to revert," she says.

The phone rings. I sit up, pull on a bathrobe and switch on the screen, expecting Sandy.

It's a guy in a serious suit. Solicitors, I think. How do they get through the screening program? I'm about to switch it off when a legal logo scrolls across the screen. A lawyer.

"Jules Morgan?" he says.

"Yes."

"We are attempting to locate Trina Coleman." He pauses. "Have you had contact with her in the last few weeks?"

"Uh, I've seen her around." From the corner of my eye, I can see Trina has frozen in place on the bed.

"Who are you representing?" I say.

"Breeton-Fugulle-Paris-Danphysics," he says. Everyone drops the "p". Biggest pharmaceutical conglomerate on the planet.

"Why are you looking for her?"

"I'm not at liberty to divulge that information," he says.

"Is there a reward?"

He must be smarter than he looks, because he says "No," and simultaneously flashes a figure on the screen. It's a lot. I wouldn't have to work as a Token for a long time.

"I don't know where she is," I say, wondering how I can let him know she's right here, right now, in my apartment.

He flashes his card to my home system. "Call me if you have any information."

I power off and Trina says, "You're thinking about turning me in, aren't you?"

"No, of course not." But of course I am. I'm thinking about how I could afford to get a better apartment. Then I think: that's a lot of money. Why do they want her so bad?

"Trina," I say. "Did you do more than take black market 'mones?"

"The thing is," she says. "I never took black market 'mones."

"What?"

"I never took any 'mones at all."

I decide to wait a little longer before calling Mr. BFD back. "What's going on, then?"

"You have to promise not to tell anyone. Okay?"

"Cross my heart."

She starts in about how she always felt like a woman trapped in a man's body, and I kind of tune out, but then I tune in again when she mentions a corporate sponsored research program about gender changing.

"Wait a minute," I say. "You're a genetic male?" What I'm thinking is: I slept with a man!

"I'm not sure," she says. "They were in the process of changing all those Y's to X's. Every cell in my body."

"True gender changing? That's not possible."

"BFD thinks it is. Targeted chromosome replacement. It makes everything else just happen on its own, without hormones or anything. I grew these fabulous breasts, and my hairy—"

"It's okay," I interrupt. "I don't need to know all the details." All I can think is: Chromosomes be damned. She was born an XY. She's ruined my record.

"It was great at first," she says. "Finally my body matched how I always thought of myself."

"So did you like women or did you like men?" I say. "I mean, before they started changing those Y's to X's?"

"Does it matter? I was finally a woman. I loved my body. But then it all started to go terribly wrong."

"Like how?"

"I started wanting to wear loose pants."

"So?"

"And wear sensible shoes!"

"Who says cargo pants look bad on a woman?" I say.

"Everyone who is fashionable," she says.

"Not me." I most definitely love my khakis. And my crew cuts. And yes, even a fanny pack looks good to me.

"A cargo lesbo! Why can't I be a lipstick—"

"All right. All right." I need to call Mr. BFD and get that reward. "How many Y's do you have left, anyway?"

"I don't know."

"Maybe if you finished the treatment—"

"And become even more unfashionable? No way! I really liked being a girl," she says. "A fashionable girl. The clothes. The heels. The makeup. Oh, god." Here we go. More weeping.

I try to head it off. "So why is the company after you?"

"Because of one of those contracts I signed. I promised to do publicity for them. TV spots. Magazines. I can't do it now. I just can't. I hate myself."

"Just go back and do the damn commercials. How hard could it be?"

"I hate flannel. But I love it!"

So did I sleep with a straight girl or a trans femme man? And does she like flannel or doesn't she? How much of her original DNA does she have left? My head is spinning.

"I put on a silk dress and I feel like a fake. I put on baggy pants and I like it. But I hate it. I hate that I like it."

Too late. The weeping has gone into waterfall mode. I ponder how to get her out of my apartment.

"I can't go home now," she says, as if reading my thoughts. "I can't go outside anymore."

"You'll have to come out to them at some point," I say. "Either that or force yourself to wear heels and motion-restricting clothes the rest of your life."

Mistake. The weeping resumes.

"Listen," I say. "I've got a brunch party to go to. Why don't you help yourself to some food. I'll be back later and we can figure out what to do."

"Thanks," she says. She wipes her eyes. "I mean it. You've been so good to me."

She won't think that for long.

*

Mr. BFD stands next to me outside a downtown café with his hands in his coat pockets. He talks straight ahead, as if we're in a spy movie and he's pretending he doesn't know me. Or maybe he's just embarrassed to be seen with someone wearing sweats and bed-head.

The smell of roasting coffee and no-foam-caramel-macchiatos wafts out each time the door slides open. Already the winter skiers are starting to thin out. There will be a lull before the summer herds arrive. That reward will come at just the right time.

"Breeton-Fugulle-Paris-Danphysics just wants to see her back safe and sound and glamorous," he says. "A little money for you, a little good publicity for us. Who's the worse?"

"Sure," I say.

"Getting a job as a Token." He rolls his eyes. "Pretty stupid. You know what I love about my job?"

No, I don't, and I don't care. But he doesn't ask if I care.

"These people are so easy to track down."

"How many are there anyway?"

But he isn't listening to me.

"They all want a free ride. Just lazy, I suppose, like all Tokens," he says. He risks a sidelong glance at me and adds as an afterthought, "No offense."

I was about to ask about that reward again, but then I change my mind.

"So what will happen to her?" I say.

He shrugs. "She broke her contract. If she comes back to LA and does the publicity, then we'll forgive the breach. Minus the fine for her actions, of course."

"A fine?"

He names a figure. Same amount as the reward. How stupid does he think I am, anyway?

"And if she doesn't?"

"No more targeted genetic treatment for her. She'll end up in a gender no-man's land. So to speak."

"I think she's already in a no-man's land," I say.

He's still looking straight ahead, barely listening to me. "She owes us," he says. "We gave her the body of her dreams, and all she does is run and hide. Typical."

"Typical of what? Typical of men who are really women who turn into last century non-fashionable lesbians?"

"What?"

"Never mind."

"Listen, it doesn't matter how she feels about her transformation. If we want her to dance, she'll dance."

"I'm not sure you'll like the way she dances now," I say.

"Are you telling me she no longer enjoys looking beautiful?"

"I'm just saying she's not fitting your definition of beautiful anymore."

"There is only one beautiful," he says. "Don't you watch television?"

He finally looks at me, and his gaze is both perplexed and condescending. "You know, maybe you should consider the program. You might look better as a man."

I grit my teeth. I manage to keep myself from responding.

"So," he says. "Are you going to tell me where she is?"

I pretend to consider for a moment. "I'll call you later."

*

When I get home, Trina is sprawled on the couch, used Kleenex surrounding her like tiny little clouds.

"Come on," I say.

"What?"

"It's time to give in to those cargo tendencies."

She tries to cover her eyes but I take her hand and pull her upright.

"I've been doing some research," I say. "It's called clothes therapy. All you need to do is give in to your butch impulses for a few days and they'll start to go away. You'll start to enjoy back-breaking stilettos and suffocating zippers once again."

"You really think so?" She looks at me with those wide,

trusting eyes.

"I know so."

"I do like the way loose shirts feel."

"Yes."

"And flats are so much more comfortable."

"Now we're talking!"

I pull her into the bedroom, fling open the closet.

Jeans and sweats and cargo pants, black slacks and button-downs for the fancy occasions. And the accessories: key chains, belts with large buckles, a few neckties. And flannel. Lots of it.

Trina rushes forward, pulls a plaid shirt to her face.

"Just give in to it, Trina," I say. "Let go."

She swoons into the flannel forest.

I back out slowly, quietly.

I use the kitchen screen to call Mr. BFD.

"She's here, at my apartment," I say, low and conspiratorial.

"I knew you'd come through for me," he says. "Flash me the address."

I get the camera uplinked and ready.

*

When Mr. BFD arrives, I have the camera on him the moment he swaggers in, red-light blinking 'live'.

"Does BFPD pharmaceutical confirm or deny the plight of Trina Coleman?" I say.

"What?" I can tell he's about to get angry, but then he sees the reality-certification-logo on the cam and changes his mind. He knows this footage is being archived and stamped as it rolls.

He looks directly into the camera. "Well, since you have that on, maybe I can explain to any potential viewers exactly what is happening here. We are here to meet Trina Coleman, a successful participant in our new gender-transformation program."

"And you want her back?"

"Of course we do. This is the real thing. Actual chromosome-changing, not just the outward sexual characteristics. Trina started out a verified XY male, went through the treatments, and emerged a stunning XX woman. And you, too, can become the woman or man of your dreams. The cost is minimal, the results guaranteed."

"Trina!" I yell. "Come out of the closet!"

Trina emerges from the bedroom. She's wearing an oversized t-shirt, out-of-date navy slacks that hang half-way down her butt, army boots and a fanny pack.

"Good god," BFD says.

"Hi Trina," I say. I give her a thumbs-up.

She looks at the camera, at Mr. BFD and then back at me. First anger glimmers in her eyes, and then understanding.

"I always loved those fanny packs," I say. "So practical."

"Turn that camera off now!" BFD says.

Trina narrows her eyes at him. Then she pulls her keys

out of her pocket and loops them on her belt.

"Nice!" I say.

"I'm getting a tattoo and a mullet this afternoon," she says.

"Butch is beautiful!" I say.

And she is beautiful. Those loose pants. Those no-nonsense boots. She is the most beautiful butch I have ever seen. Her regal air is back. Trina is a strong, proud, boot-wearing goddess.

"Well?" I say. "You still want her for those publicity spots?"

"You can't show up in LA with a fanny pack," BFD says to Trina. "I'll lose my job."

I lower the camera, switch it off.

"Well, then," Trina says. "How about you explain to the company why I can't do those commercials?"

BFD scowls, looks like he is about to say something, thinks better of it. He heads for the door, then turns at the last minute. "You keep that footage archived or the deal is off," he says.

"Fine by me," Trina says.

He turns to me. "And you're not getting any reward."

I shrug. "I guess I'll just keep working as a Token. Easy money, you know."

He slams the door as he leaves.

Trina sinks onto the couch. "Good riddance," she says.

"What about finishing the program?" I say.

She shrugs. "I'm starting to like myself just the way I am."

"Not everyone can be lipstick," I say.

She smiles. "You must think I'm a total jerk."

The funny thing is, I don't.

"You're okay," I say. "For someone with a few Y's."

Heart of Darkness, Heart of Light

"What is your name?" the woman asked.

She had thick dark hair held back with a silver clasp and two gold bracelets that clinked together when she shifted the pliers in her hands.

Marlow tried to lift himself up and found his wrists and ankles shackled to the legs of the cot. The ceiling was green canvas. On all sides the walls sloped outward, defining a large windowless room. The air smelled of mud.

A flap in the tent opened briefly and Marlow caught sight of trees, a loamy forest floor. The sun angling through the cloth doorway blinded him for a moment. He blinked and saw that the woman had pulled a cart of medical equipment next to his cot. She attached electrodes to Marlow's head, set a metal band against his chest.

"Have I been hurt?" he asked.

His head ached. The last thing he remembered was crawling through brambles in the dusk, squinting through the low hanging branches to locate the others in his unit. How had he managed to pass out during routine practice maneuvers at the base in Munich?

She opened a drawer in the cart. Inside, scalpels and razor blades lay in neat rows next to ordinary household tools: hammers, screwdrivers, ball point pens.

He felt a warning shiver across the base of his scalp. He tried the shackles but they held firm. "Who are you?" he said. "Are you a nurse?"

She set the pliers down, considered, then picked them up again. Vice grip locking pliers, DeWitt Manufacturing. He had a pair at his parent's house in New Jersey.

"I've never been in combat," he said. He felt a bead of sweat coalesce under his right eyebrow. "I only joined the army three months ago."

All he had ever done was train and drill and train some more in Germany. He had never even seen Iraq or Afghanistan or any of those places.

"I don't know anything," he said. "I swear I don't."

The woman didn't meet his eye. She clamped the pliers over his index finger, tightened the locknut.

At first there was just the tickling warning of pressure on

his fingernail, then a jab of true pain, and then crushing agony. The woman flicked the release, and the pliers fell to the ground. Marlow panted. She leaned toward him, traced a slow finger across his forehead.

"What is your name," she said.

*

Marlow stood up straight. He felt strong and alive. He felt more sure of himself than ever before in his life. The only problem was that he was handcuffed, taken into custody by his own army.

Two guards stood on either side of him. They had brought him to this large hospital room with painted concrete walls and a bed in one corner surrounded by doctors and monitors.

A small, uniformed man detached himself from the group of doctors. His badge read Lt. Spencer. He carried a laptop and would not meet Marlow's eyes.

"What happened inside that tent?" Spencer said.

"What tent?"

Spencer opened his laptop. "Don't play games," he said. "We need to know what happened. We can help you."

"I don't need your help," Marlow said.

Spencer turned and indicated the hospital bed.

Marlow focused on the figure in the bed. He had expected this, but it was still a shock to see that face. The man's eyes were closed, his pale hair plastered to his forehead with sweat. The man was Marlow's physical twin.

"Weakling," Marlow said with disgust.

The doctors looked at each other.

The female doctor spoke softly into the man's ear, and Marlow's twin gnashed his teeth in response.

"We have him in simulation therapy," Spencer continued. "To make him remember. We could do the same to you."

Marlow shrugged.

"Obviously you know him," the lieutenant said. "Is he your twin?"

Marlow began to laugh.

*

When Marlow woke up on Pluto, white clouds spelled words against a velvet purple sky. Go Home, they said. He wanted nothing more than to go home, and he had never trusted a purple sky, but he had a mission to accomplish.

He suited up and waited for the commands.

"Marlow, do you read?" Control said.

"Yes."

"Do you know where you are?" Control said.

"The edge of the solar system," Marlow answered. He scanned the sky. His sun was a tiny pinprick of golden light against the velvet.

"You need to head in, Marlow, towards the center. Find the tent."

The mention of a tent made Marlow's heart cold, but he

knew he had to follow orders. He climbed the ladder into the rocket ship and sat in the single padded seat. Panels covered with switches and numeric displays surrounded him, a single oval window overhead.

"Three, two, one," Control said. "Lift-off."

*

Marlow lay on his cot, half-awake, half seeing the green canvas overhead. He no longer cared that he had soiled his pants, that he had sweat through his shirt many times already, that he hadn't slept in three days.

The woman played with the medical equipment just outside his field of view. He heard beeps and the clicks of knobs turning. He barely felt where the IV entered his forearm. That pain was insignificant compared to other pain he had recently experienced.

Men stood outside smoking. He could hear their voices, smell their clove cigarettes. Occasionally a silhouette flickered against the wall of the tent. They spoke in Arabic and German and English. He heard "axis of evil" very clearly in English, and then laughing.

The woman approached his cot, and he felt his body begin to tremble.

She had so many instruments. Already he was familiar with the hammer, the band saw blade, the scalpel. She used ethanol in unusual ways.

Today when she knelt next to him, she looked him in the

eye.

"My name is Fatima," she said. She draped her arm across his chest like a lover.

"You will talk to me," she whispered in his ear. Her accent was very faint.

Yes, he thought, I will talk.

He spoke to Fatima. He told her everything he knew, and then when he couldn't remember anything more about his army and country, he told her pieces of his childhood, and scraps of memory and half-remembered dreams. He wanted to keep on talking forever. It was cathartic.

His soul was laid bare, and he was cleansed. She listened with the rapt attention of a lover. She was his psychiatrist, his confidant, his soul-mate. She was ferocious in her silence.

*

"They tortured you," Lt. Spencer said.

"She tortured me," Marlow corrected, then regretted giving anything away.

"Why?" Spencer asked. "Who was she?"

Behind Spencer the doctors worked on Marlow's prone twin in the hospital bed, pretending not to listen.

Spencer would not let Marlow sit down. Marlow did not mind. He had experienced far worse. Spencer could never do to him what Fatima had done.

"I don't know," Marlow said.

But he did know, and he was grateful. Fatima had set him

free.

"What *do* you know?" Spencer said, a hint of exasperation in his voice.

Marlow knew pain. He knew it could swell and ebb like waves on the ocean. Pain could dance across nerve endings in staccato stabs or feathery strokes. He knew about throbbing aches and razor-sharp bites; pain that grew intolerable in one instant, then receded to a shadow the next; he had known the steady hum of constant pain at the edge of his awareness, like air against his skin.

Spencer raised his eyes from his laptop and watched Marlow. Marlow returned the gaze until Spencer finally looked away.

"When we found you outside Heidelberg," Spencer said, "you had killed five people, two of them children."

Children, yes, Marlow thought. So innocent.

"We speculate they released you somewhere in the Black Forest, and you made your way to the outskirts, where you first stole food, and then began to kill."

"Of course I took food," Marlow said. "I was hungry."

"Why did you kill those people?"

Marlow shrugged. Wasn't it obvious? But Spencer only waited.

"Because I could," Marlow said finally.

*

After he had passed Saturn, Marlow began to hear

whispers from outside.

"I hear people talking," he said.

"What are they saying?" Control said.

The voices grew louder, then receded just beyond his range of hearing. They were speaking a mishmash of English, German, and Arabic.

A sudden flare of memory: his mother pinning a small American flag to his collar. He knew she didn't want him to join the army. She was afraid for him, afraid of what war might do to him. He smiled to show her he would be all right. He wished he had told her he loved her.

"What are the voices saying?" Control asked again.

"They're too far away," Marlow said.

"Follow them. Find the tent."

Marlow scanned the instrument panels. Numbers scrolled furiously by. "Mars," he decided. "They're on Mars."

The panels chirped and winked; the rocket descended through oranges and yellows, touched down on the swollen face of Mars.

The hatch wheezed open onto swirling red fog.

The voices were louder here. The air carried the smell of cloves.

"Who would have thought Mars would be so foggy," Marlow said.

"Find the tent," Control said.

Marlow walked into the fog. His feet eased into pliant red sand.

A man's voice spoke clearly from somewhere just ahead, "Why do they always use women?"

Another answered, "Because they bring out the bad in men."

There was laughing, and then coughing. They shouldn't smoke so much, Marlow thought. Even clove cigarettes could kill you.

Marlow felt a tremor in his gut. He didn't want to see the men. He didn't want to listen to them anymore. He reached out his hand and felt the cold metallic surface of his rocket. He climbed inside, shivering.

"I can't do it," he said.

He knew what Control would say next. "You have to continue on."

What was next? Earth. But he knew they wouldn't let him stop there.

*

Fatima leaned over him, and Marlow realized that she was cleaning his wounds. Every cut had been precise, and she had sterilized her tools before using them.

"Why are you doing this?" he asked. His throat was dry and the words came out barely comprehensible, but she understood.

"My whole life," she said, "I have seen children killed by your military. Drone attacks in Afghanistan, bombs in Hebron. My husband and three children were killed by men in

Baghdad." She paused. "Men just like you."

"Not like me," Marlow managed. "I wouldn't kill children."

"Yes, you would."

Marlow stretched for something, anything that would convince her. She was talking to him, and there was a chance that he could get her to stop the pain, even for just a little while.

"I'm sorry about your husband and children," he said. He truly was. "But that wasn't me. I'm a good man."

"Part of you is good," she said, and he felt a tiny flare of hope. "But part of you is bad. I will show you."

Fatima reached for the scalpel, and he knew then that nothing he said would stop her. Her torture was for a reason other than information, because he had no information to give her. The thought made his chest ache with fear, and he wished for the thousandth time that he were already dead.

*

"Any progress?" Spencer leaned over the shoulders of the doctors, who still stared at Marlow's twin and the monitors above him. One was speaking into a microphone.

"He thinks he's on Mars," the female said.

"Get him to talk!" Spencer's face had turned red.

The guards next to Marlow eased forward, their attention diverted to Spencer. Marlow smiled. It suddenly became clear what he was to do. If the one on his right turned just a little more, he would be able to reach the gun.

*

Marlow sped right past his beautiful blue-and-white home, and headed for Venus.

The rocket landed in the middle of a pine forest, branches cracking against the hull.

Marlow padded into the forest, green needles cushioning his steps.

The voices grew louder. He peeked past a tree, nose inches from the peeling bark. The men stood in a knot just outside the entrance to a tent. He knew what was happening inside that tent. He wanted to run away from it and never come back, but his legs felt very weak. There was a faint droning in the background.

"Concentrate, Marlow. What are the men saying?"

He focused his attention back to the men. Cigarette smoke wafted away from them in gray clouds. They wore khaki pants and polo shirts. They seemed too thin to be terrorists.

The droning emerged from the forest as a black sedan.

The men glanced down, around, everywhere except at the woman who got out of the car, then disappeared into the tent.

One of the men crushed his cigarette out on the heel of his boot. "I feel sorry for them," he said, and Marlow wasn't sure if he was talking about the woman or the man who lay in that tent.

Marlow turned and ran as fast as he could, until his lungs burned and his legs crumpled beneath him at the base of his rocket.

He climbed in, pulled the hatch closed.

"No," he said. "No more."

But he knew what Control would say next. "You have to go further," Control said.

The acceleration shoved Marlow into the seat as the rocket lifted. There was only one planet left between him and the sun.

*

"Evil lies at the heart of all men," Fatima said.

She touched the point of a scalpel just under his left eye, and Marlow felt the muscles of his face tighten in response.

"I'm not evil." Even as he said it, Marlow felt hate washing over him. He wanted to reach up and strangle Fatima.

No, he didn't just want to kill her. He wanted to hurt her. He wanted her to feel the same kind of pain he felt. And when he had raped and beaten and strangled her, he would kill the complicit men outside, who stood smoking and talking like nothing was happening inside this tent.

Fatima traced the scalpel across his face and down his neck to a point just over his collarbone.

She leaned over him, looked straight down into his eyes. "I'm sorry I have to do this to you," she said.

In that instant he was in love with her again, her beautiful thick hair, her kiln-dark skin, her magnificent cold eyes. She was sorry that she had to do this. Terrible for him, but terrible for her as well. They were in this together, and he had never felt closer to anyone.

The knife bit into his collarbone, and Marlow felt his blood well up, and he hated her again, more than he had ever hated anyone or anything.

Fatima cut the remaining tatters of Marlow's clothes from him. She spread grease on metal disks and placed them on Marlow's chest, his hips, his temple, his thighs. She ran thin wires from a machine behind the cot to the disks. She placed a cold band across Marlow's forehead, something soft over his ears, a thermal blanket over his torso. She adjusted his IV.

She looked at him from the corner of her eye.

"Our time is almost over," she said.

There was something different in her eyes now.

Fear, he thought. That was what she felt. Fear. Of him?

"Think of the power that one man can have," she said. "In America, one man in Oklahoma killed over a hundred people with a simple home-made bomb. In Bosnia, one sniper killed three hundred and thirty seven people in one week."

"Why are you telling me this?"

"I'm going to set you free now," she said.

*

Mercury, the final planet, lit up on one side by the nearness of a white-hot sun, dark on the other with the icy black of space.

The LED display below the window read, "Here Be Monsters".

Marlow began to run as soon as the rocket landed. He ran away from the voices. The ground was orange and parched and went on for miles.

He was already out of breath when he realized the ground had become a soft mossy forest floor, the sky a canopy of branches. Patches of blue filtered lazily through.

He fell to his knees in front of a tent. The men smoking out front ignored him. They had their attention on the tent flap.

Screams came from inside that tent. A man and a woman, both screaming.

"No," he said. He didn't want to remember. He sobbed into the mossy pine-needle floor and remembered.

*

"Here we go," Fatima said, and rotated a surgeon's light above his body.

He squinted against the light, turned his head. Above the churn of machines he heard music: what sounded like violins played in the twelve-tone scale. He shook his head, but the earphones held tight.

Fatima switched on another machine, and he felt a humming through the cot. His body spasmed as an electrical shock coursed through him. Hate sputtered alive and rose to the top of his mind like fat in boiling water. There was an instant of blackness, and he felt his entire being reach for her. He wanted nothing more than to wrap his hands around her throat.

The blackness receded. He knew now what would happen.

"No," he said. "Don't do this."

The music grew louder. Another jolt of current. His back arched, and he began to feel the tearing.

His chest was splitting. Not just his chest, his entire being was being torn apart. Every molecule, ripped in two.

Fatima brought a key from her pocket. She opened the handcuffs on his ankles and wrists. The blanket slid from his chest.

The current flashed through him once more, and he saw double: back flat against the cot, squinting up into the light, and at the same time sitting up, reaching for Fatima. She stood still, and he saw her eyes widen, though she didn't run.

He held his hands before his face, willing the nightmare to stop. But when he pulled his hands away, the other Marlow still stood there.

There were two of him now.

And Marlow understood that the man standing over the cot was also Marlow; he embodied every dark impulse Marlow had ever felt and suppressed. He would maim and torture and he would enjoy it. He would do all the terrible things Marlow had ever fleetingly wanted to do.

"No," he said. But it was too late.

He watched the man that had been part of him pick up the handcuff and swing it into Fatima's face. She fell back against the canvas, and he felt the tent sway in response.

Marlow retched over the side of the cot as the other Marlow beat Fatima. The air was bloated with the thud of metal meeting flesh.

The violins wailed their accompaniment to her screams.

When he looked up again, Fatima was dead.

The other Marlow dropped the handcuff and strode from the tent.

*

Marlow watched his weakling twin thrash in the hospital bed.

"His heart rate—" one of the doctors said. The others gathered over the console.

"What's happening?" Spencer demanded.

"He's remembering the moment I left him," Marlow said. He gave his full attention to the lieutenant. He liked that the lieutenant flinched.

"We shared the same body once, me and him," Marlow said.

"That's impossible," Spencer said.

Marlow laughed. He still remembered with a visceral thrill the moment Fatima had released him.

Spencer looked back at the hospital bed. The guards were intent on the thrashing twin, and Marlow was close enough.

He jumped at the guard, thrust his fingers into the man's throat and pulled the gun from the belt as the guard staggered backwards. He shot the guard before he had finished falling.

Spencer blocked the other guard's line-of-sight, and Marlow fired through both of them at once. Then he shot the doctors in turn, the crack of the gun echoing sharply from the hard walls. All except the female doctor.

Too easy, Marlow thought. It was amazing what one could accomplish without the burden of conscience.

It was suddenly very quiet, the only sound the muttering of the man in the hospital bed. The female doctor stood blinking stupidly at him. He would enjoy her later.

He dropped the gun, found the guard's keys on his belt, uncuffed himself.

He approached the female.

"Against the wall," he said.

The woman backed up until she was pressed flat against the far wall.

"Kneel," he commanded.

The woman knelt, her hands clasped in front of her chest, trembling.

"Don't move," he said.

He would kill the weakling first.

He leaned over the bed and pressed his hands against Marlow's throat. The man's body tightened in response. He pressed his thumbs into Marlow's windpipe, and felt the body begin to convulse.

The tickling of wind on the back of his neck was the only warning he had. By the time he lifted his head, the woman had sprinted past him. He began to follow, but something tugged at him. It was Marlow, rising from the hospital bed. Marlow held Marlow in place as the woman leaned over the guard's body and picked up the gun.

Marlow grappled with his double, unable to push him aside.

The woman approached, and Marlow saw the pain and anger and fear in her eyes coming together in cathartic comprehension of the ridiculous ease with which she could take Marlow's life. Power and revenge, an addictive blend. He knew well what could blossom from the fertile ground of pain. He saw that she felt it, and he finally truly understood what Fatima had done. Like a chain reaction, one atom crashed into another and freed more atoms, cascading on until the reaction was unstoppable.

Marlow struggled against Marlow, that weak man who could not understand the joy of power, the man who held him back against defending himself.

Marlow embraced Marlow, the man who had lost his tie to humanity.

They both understood they were insane. They both heard the shot that exploded through their bodies, tearing the fragile walls of cells and capillaries in a final frenzied dance of blood with blood.

*

The rocket sped through the dark night, the blackest yet because it was so close to the heart of light, his sun. The sun reached out for Marlow in fiery arcs through the boundary between light and dark. Marlow realized there was no rocket, no Control, and there never had been. The earth and all the planets and the rest of the universe fell away. There was just this moment, the core of him. I will not be afraid, he thought. Into the heart of pulsating light he went, and saw no darkness there.

All Souls Day

That jerk Manuel was blocking her parking spot, just standing there grinning like he was really funny. He wasn't. Connie inched the car toward Manuel's knees.

"Hey!" he said. He jumped out of the way. His baseball cap flew off.

Connie rolled down her window so hard the little plastic handle almost popped off in her hand. "Get out of my way."

Manuel picked up his cap. "Why are you always so mad?"

She parked, got out, and slammed the door.

Only a mile away San Francisco's office buildings rose like tall sentries into the clouds, guardians of suits and plush offices.

But here was where asphalt and steel became gravel and barbed-wire, Armani gave way to flannel shirts, white faces to brown. Here was where those self-righteous pricks had to come in person into the world of litter and oil stains, and Connie never got tired of telling them no, they only took cash, and yes, it really was three hundred dollars a day for impoundment. Too bad, buddy. Thought you were too important to have your car towed? Well, maybe you shouldn't have parked in a no-parking zone.

Manuel beat the cap against his jeans, put it on backwards. "I got tickets for the Day of the Dead fiesta tonight," he said. "You want to go?"

She gave him a hard stare. "How many times do I have to tell you? I don't do any Mexican stuff. I'm not ever going to any fiesta with you. Ever."

They always could tell she was Hispanic, even though she went by Connie now, not Consuelo. Her hair was glossy black, and her skin a deep brown, thanks to a father she had never known. But she didn't speak any Spanish except a few choice phrases useful for shocking men. And why on earth would anyone want to go to a Day of the Dead festival? The dead were dead. Let them be.

Manuel shrugged. "Brad dared me. He said if I talk you into it he'll give me one hundred dollars. What say you go and we split it?"

She turned away, kicked aside a Styrofoam cup that had

nestled against the trailer overnight and unlocked the door. She flipped on the dispatch radio, picked up the receipt log, settled behind the particle-board desk.

Someone entered only a few minutes later.

"What kind of car?" she said, not looking up. Her head still throbbed from the previous night's drinking. The binder indicated that two SUVs had been towed, three small cars, and one hummer. She bet the hummer jerk would try to buy her off. All the rich guys thought they could act sweet to Connie, slip her a twenty, get their car for free.

The man hadn't moved. "Consuelo," he said.

She jerked her head up.

It was impossible, but there he was. Elliot. Unmistakable delicate oval face. Long blond hair pulled back in a pony tail. Eyes pale blue to the point of white. Exactly the same except that he was human-sized. His hands extended from too-long sleeves, long and bony. Human-sized hands.

She opened her mouth to speak, found she couldn't breathe. Elliot. After all these years. Elliot. He was dead. He was tiny. It was impossible.

She heard a scratching sound, realized it was her hand inching across the desk, trying to reach the phone.

"It's been a long time," Elliot said. He turned and left the office.

The bells on the door chimed. Cold air puffed against her ankles. The sounds from outside came slowly back to her: a dog barking, Brad yelling at someone.

She had spent years convincing herself Elliot was not real. Elliot was a figment. A child's fantasy. But here he was again. Real. Large.

She got up slowly, carefully, looked out the window. He was walking toward the garage.

She was going crazy for sure. Certifiable. Manuel would call her Loco Connie and she would be sent to the loony bin.

Elliot disappeared into the garage. Connie opened the door and followed him.

*

"Consuelo!" Her mother's voice rang out in the still night air. Nights like this the air was so cold Consuelo thought maybe she could open her mouth and eat it like a popsicle. It was too cold to snow, according to Grady, her mom's new boyfriend. Too cold to be outside. But Grady was inside, so Consuelo would play outside, no matter how much her mother called, no matter how cold she got, even if she froze up like an icicle and never thawed out again which would be okay because then Grady wouldn't want to touch her because he would get frostbite and his fingers would fall off.

The back door slammed shut. Her mother was angry. Good.

It was then she heard the noise. It was a high-pitched squeaking like a tape-recorder played on fast forward, except that it also sounded like people singing. She looked all around. No one else shared the patch of prickly dead grass between the brick apartment buildings. The trees pointed thin naked limbs upwards. Her breath misted the air. She heard the sounds again and realized they had come from somewhere near her feet, underneath her apartment building.

The wood lattice was starting to rot in places, and she was able to pull a few pieces aside and peer into the small space. The basement was only a few feet high, with pipes running over the packed dirt. She crawled in, pushing aside a yellowing newspaper. The place smelled old, like her grandfather's breath.

There. On top of one of the pipes. There was a swarm of little people, only as tall as her hand. At first she thought maybe they were toys, but then she saw they were talking and singing, and some of them were fluttering into the air and then back down again.

She inched toward them on her elbows and knees.

When she got close, one of them saw her and yelled a warning, and they flew in all directions like a giant swarm of flies.

She swung her hand through the air and caught one. His skin was pale, his hair long and blond and braided like a girl's. His wings fluttered against her palm, colorful and delicate. He looked like the pictures of fairies she had seen once in a book.

He said something in his high-pitched voice, some language she didn't know.

"I'm going to call you Elliot," she said. She liked that he was small.

Her mom had told her fairies didn't exist. Then again, her mom was wrong about a lot of things.

*

Connie stood in the garage entrance. Elliot was no where inside. He must have walked right past Brad and out the back door.

"What's up, Connie," Brad said. He picked up a wrench, worked at something in one of the tow engines.

I just saw a ghost, she could say. A dead fairy. Someone I killed a long time ago.

Instead she said, "Nothing. Slow morning."

"Well then, get back to the office," he said. "Don't bug me."

"A-hole."

"That's my Connie."

She didn't want to go back to the office. Even Brad was better than being alone. She looked at the oil-stained concrete floor, racks of tools against the walls. A girl playing in one corner. She looked again. No, she hadn't imagined it.

"Who's that?" she said.

Brad pulled a hose out from under the hood, examined it. "Manuel's daughter. Apparently the babysitter quit today."

"No kids allowed in here," she said.

"In case you've forgotten," Brad said, squaring his shoulders and finally looking at her, "I am the boss. Maria is not bothering anyone." He turned and called over to the girl.

"You'll be quiet, won't you, Maria?"

Maria looked up, nodded. She went back to tearing apart a stuffed animal. Cotton stuffing surrounded her like scattered clouds.

Connie walked over to the child, squatted down.

"That's a nice looking penguin," she said.

"He's not a penguin. He's a puffin." The puffin was lumpy, half his innards missing. Maria had Manuel's high forehead, his dark, thick hair. She didn't have his easy smile.

"Okay." Connie tried on her best smile. Not that the kid was looking at her. "What's his name?"

"Puffin."

"Great name," Brad said from behind her.

Maria abruptly shook the puffin, raising a small cloud of cotton and dirt into the air.

"Bad," Maria said. "Bad. Bad. Bad. Puffin." She punctuated each word with a slap of the puffin's head on the concrete.

Connie felt an odd tingling at the base of her neck. She stood up and faced Brad, now leaning casually against one of the nearby tow trucks. He was trying not to laugh.

"You're going to let this kid stay in the garage all day?"

He shrugged. "What's it to you? I thought I told you to get back to work."

She looked down at the girl. "You want to come play in the office?" she asked.

"She's fine in here," Brad said.

"It's cold."

"I said she's fine." Brad's eyes narrowed, daring her.

Connie felt Maria watch her as she walked back through the high garage door. She felt the small dark eyes on the back of her head. Not her responsibility, she thought. Stupid kids. What a nuisance.

*

"You want to see my muscles?" Grady said.

Consuelo shook her head no, but Grady was standing so close she could smell his sweat, and anyway he was already pulling off his shirt. All she could think about was how his forearms looked like giant meaty chicken legs as they angled down into the waistband of her skirt and how if she cried she might wake up her mother who was asleep in the next room after doing a double shift. Or maybe her mother would wake up and not care and that would be worse so she said nothing at all.

The phone rang and Grady looked up and her mother's sleepy voice said, "Grady? Can you get that?" and that was enough time for Consuelo to wiggle out of Grady's hands and run out the back door and downstairs and squeeze under the apartment building where no one could fit except her and Elliot.

Elliot was where she had left him in the overturned strawberry carton with the big rock on top. He was curled up in a ball, but he sat up when she crawled over to him. She took off the rock, lifted up the cage.

She wondered if he looked the same as Grady under that robe. Her hand snaked out before she had fully made up her mind to look. His legs dangled from her fist. She tugged at his robe. He tugged back. But she was big and he was little and she could do whatever she wanted. She pulled the robe off. He did look like Grady, only in miniature. He was so small she could reach over and pull off his thing if she wanted.

But she didn't want to touch his thing so instead she tugged on his wings.

He said something in a language she didn't understand, and then he said, "No. No!"

He struggled in her hands, and then he let out a gasp. One wing was half torn off and he started to scream. He was small and his lungs were small and he couldn't make much noise. A tiny pin scratching a tiny chalkboard. No one would hear him.

Consuelo tugged and tugged and the wing came off, and she held up the bloody thing and felt bad and strong all at once. He shivered and cried. She put him back down in his cage and put the rock on top.

"There," she said. "Don't you forget who's in charge here." She had heard that in a movie once. She liked the way it sounded.

*

Connie stood outside the garage, reluctant to go back to the office.

For a moment she thought she heard someone whimpering. No, just a trick of the wind. And here was Manuel's truck heading up the road in a cloud of gravel-dust. He was towing a rusted twenty-year-old piece of crap Chevy, barely recognizable. Probably an abandoned car. No money in that. Brad wouldn't be happy.

Manuel pulled through the gate, a Mariachi band blaring from his radio. He turned down the volume when she approached his window.

"Tell me about the Day of the Dead," she said.

He straightened. "You want to go?"

"No. I just want to know what it's about."

"You honor your dead. You give food and offerings. Lots of good food. You make masks to scare them away at the end of the night."

"Do you ever see them?"

"See who?"

"The dead."

"Some people say they do."

"Do they change size?"

"What are you talking about?"

"Like if they are small when they die, say, a child. Can they come back as spirits any size, like adult size?"

"I don't know." He gave her a look. "You feeling okay?"

"Of course I'm okay."

"Just asking. Don't be so mad." Something near the office caught his eye. "Hey, we have a customer?"

Connie's heart flailed against its cage. She knew before she even turned to look. Elliot. He stood just outside the trailer door. He beckoned to her.

*

When she got under the house, Elliot was dead. He was curled up tight like a bug, his robe bunched up under him, and when she poked him with her finger, his body was stiff and cold. There was a darker spot in the dirt where he had bled from his torn-off wing.

She stared at his body a long time. Something stirred inside her, something large and dark and frightening.

"I'm not sorry," she said. Her voice fell flat in the dark space, seeped away into the ground. She was strong. She was in control. She had shown him who was in charge.

Finally, she dug into the half-frozen ground, her fingernails tearing, until she had a small hole. She placed his curled up body in the hole, with his robe on top, and then she filled it in with dirt.

No one would ever know. No one had to know. Who would care, anyway, about someone so small?

*

Connie followed Elliot into the office, and she knew she was going to die. What else could he be here for?

He stood over her, tall and strong. And then she understood: Elliot had been getting bigger through all the years since she killed him. He had grown and grown, just like she had, until he was human sized. All those times she had seen shadows in doorways, had felt someone staring at her from a dark window; that was Elliot. That was Elliot growing and waiting and watching and finally getting big enough to confront her, just like she had imagined confronting Grady through all those years, wishing she could kill him.

But when she was finally big enough, she found she was a coward. She had never told her mother. She had never gone to the police. She had never tried to find Grady.

"You took me away from my people," he said.

She couldn't look at him.

"You tore off my wing."

The truth of the matter was that she understood Grady. She knew about the satisfaction of causing pain, that exquisite combination of self-loathing and power.

She heard that whimpering again. She glanced through the dirty window, saw no one in the lot.

Elliot shrugged off his coat. One wing unfurled from his naked back, all gossamer beauty. The other side was a ragged scar.

"Consuelo," Elliot said. "There is unfinished business."

She imagined her arm tearing from her body. Was that what he had come to do? Or to kill her outright?

"Please be quick," she said.

"You need to do something," he said. "Go to her."

"What?"

"The child. Maria. Go to her."

The whimpering. She could hear it again. She didn't know what he meant. And then she did.

She pushed past Elliot, fled the office. Her feet slid in the gravel.

Brad was not in the garage. Neither was Maria. Traces of cotton stuffing littered the floor. Connie followed the trail out the back of the garage, into the rows of cars.

On one side was a line of rusty never-claimed junkers. On the other was the night's take, newer cars.

The whimpering grew louder.

She caught a glimpse of white cotton drifting three cars up, bullied by the wind. She followed it, ducked between the hummer and a Lexus SUV.

Brad was crouched on the ground next to Maria. The girl sat with her back to a tire.

Brad stood up suddenly when he caught sight of Connie. The buttons of his jeans were undone.

Connie froze. Her chest tightened. Her fingernails pressed sharp into her palms. And there just above the nearest car was Elliot, grown even taller and paler and thinner still, stretched out like a scar against the grey sky. Brave Elliot. Elliot had grown up and come back to find her. He was going to kill her, so it didn't matter what she did now.

Brad buttoned his jeans casually, grinned at Connie.

"What's up?" he said. He strolled toward her.

She waited until he was close, was going to walk right by

like he hadn't a care in the world, and then she swung. Her fist connected with his temple in a satisfying thud, and she felt all those fine bones in her knuckles crunch together.

Brad staggered, rubbed his temple. His surprise turned to something darker. He closed the distance, grabbed her throat and forced her back against the hummer. He was a lot stronger than she was, and when she struggled she felt her right shoulder wrenching from the socket and all she could think was this was like the pain she had caused Elliot, that's what it would have felt like to lose a wing.

"Elliot," she said. "I'm sorry. I'm so sorry."

"What the fuck?" Brad let go for just a moment, and it was enough time for her to reach up and grab his ears and pull his head down and her knee up at the same time. His head snapped back and then he collapsed. Blood flowed from his mouth and he gagged and spit something into the dirt. The tip of his tongue.

Footsteps pounded gravel and suddenly Manuel was kneeling next to Maria. "What happened?" he said. He looked at Brad, back to Connie. "What did you do?"

Brad raised himself up on his knees, then pushed upright, holding his hand to his mouth.

"That bitch attacked me," he said. Connie saw his eyes shift to Maria, saw him daring her. She saw the fear on Maria's face, saw the moment she decided not to tell, because Brad was a grown-up and even if other grown-ups believed her, Brad could come back for her. Connie knew about fear and retaliation and keeping quiet.

Suddenly she was slipping, falling back into that cold brick apartment. She was small again like Maria. She was lying in a dark room and clutching a sheet to her chin and she was hurt where Grady had put his thing, but she would not cry. She never cried. She hadn't cried when she broke her arm in fourth grade and she never cried when Grady touched her and she would never cry. Ever.

But someone was crying now. Connie blinked, saw Brad and Manuel and Maria all staring at the sky.

Elliot's wing had grown back, beautiful and delicate and covered with soft down like the fuzz on a peach and she suddenly wanted more than anything for him to be able to fly. Even as she wished it, he spread his wings so wide they shadowed the whole line of cars. They arched red and yellow and green across the sky.

Brad fell back down to his knees. Manuel and Maria stared, mouths open.

"It's an angel," Maria said.

Elliot's wings angled up and over the clouds and a strip of blue sky revealed itself. Elliot smiled down at her. Connie felt a loosening inside her, a tiny fissure opening up in her core.

She knew what she needed to do.

She swallowed hard. Her throat ached.

"Brad assaulted Maria," she said. She kept her voice level. She spoke to Manuel.

Manuel tore his eyes from the sky.

"What?" he said.

"He sexually assaulted your daughter."

And then Elliot lifted into the sky behind Manuel, beautiful and silent and finally free, and she felt the echo of his flight in her bones, felt the drawing upward of courage and truth from the very black of the earth and transforming into all the colors of the world. His wings took him up and into that strip of blue, until he was a speck and then he was gone.

When Connie looked down again, Manuel had Brad's shirtfront bunched in his fist.

"I'll call the police," she said.

Manuel nodded. He let go of Brad, pushed him back.

"If you ever come near her again I will kill you," he said to Brad. "You'll be dead. Do you understand?"

Brad spit blood at Manuel's feet. "Crazy," he said. He glanced at the sky again. "Fucking crazy." His face was pale. His hands shook when he wiped his mouth. He walked away.

Manuel sat on the ground next to Maria, put an arm around her, hugged her. "He'll never hurt you again," he said. "Never." And then he spoke to her in Spanish, low and gentle, and Connie didn't need to know the language to hear love.

Maria looked up. "Why are you crying?" she said.

"I'm not crying," Connie said. She reached up, felt the wetness on her own cheeks. Maria had not been the one whimpering, either.

"My dad says it's okay to cry," Maria said.

Connie smiled. "Your dad is a good man."

"What's the matter with you?" Manual said, but he was smiling. "So nice all of a sudden. And what was that thing in the sky?"

She shrugged. "It's the Day of the Dead. Remember?"

Maria reached over to her flattened puffin, pulled him to her chest.

"Puffin got hurt," she said. "Can you make him better?"

Both Maria and Manuel looked at Connie.

"Yes," she said. "I think we can make him better."

Mamafield

Mama holds us close, long roots circled deep.

Safe with me, she sprays. Her scents hang just a moment then float thin with breeze.

I'm at edge of mamacircle, so I see him best. *Leaver*, I breathe.

Don't say name, Mama warns.

He's just a black speck under far trees, so I open all eyes upstalk to see better.

The speck moves into full sun, and I see he has strong roots furrowing earth and a big full sunhead.

We pull close in to mamacenter.

Why he back? Sister Third asks.

Where he go? Brother Second sprays.

Why he leave? a new bud asks. She hasn't heard the story.

Mama stays quiet. She scents sadness and fear.

My roots find a rock deep down and grip it tight. I only know Leaver through storytime. Evil Leaver. Betrayer. He talks to birds. He leaves Mama. But now he's back.

*

Leaver takes his time. His roots dig strong, raise long high furrows. His stalk sways forward, back, forward.

Sunsoak time is over. Bug scents fade. Still he closes in. I see sky lights when he is close enough to scent.

Hello. Like he hasn't been gone so long. Like he didn't hurt Mama so bad.

We hold scents tight.

His sunhead is wide, leaves browned at the tips, like he's soaked too long.

He moves closer. New bud squeezes stalk eyes shut.

But Leaver doesn't scent angry or mean. He scents excitement.

Long trip, he scents, and then he sprays something new. I don't know what it means. It hints adventure.

So many new soils, he sprays. *I story.*

Mama won't let him story, no way, I think.

High steep hills full of stone, he scents. *Water rushing in rivers impossible to cross.*

Why then? Mama's scents are ringed with tension.

The wonder! His scent is thick. *The huge wide land. Beautiful deep soils, perfect for seeds.*

No one leaves mamafield, Mama scents. *No one leaves Mama.*

Mamafield depletes, Leaver scents. What he says is true. I can feel it at the edge of mamacircle. The soil is better further out. More food, more worms.

Mamafield is always home. She makes Leaver sound wrong.

Will run out someday.

Someday is never, she scents.

Someday sooner than tomorrow.

You spoke to birds. I've never smelled such anger from Mama.

Leaver doesn't answer. He migrates his eyes away, starts digging outcircle.

You leave! Mama sprays thick in the air. *You leave now.*

We pull roots away from Leaver. He pulls outcircle and even further. He moves until I can't scent him anymore. Sun dips below edge of mamafield, so I close stalk eyes. Maybe he stops, maybe he goes.

What he do? We crowd close, fill the dirt of his passage.

He leaves home. He leaves mamacenter.

But we know there's more to the story.

He talks to birds.

Everyone is so still I can smell the hopping of a night bug.

Tell, whispers new bud. *Tell, tell.*

I feel mama's roots around my own, guarding, protecting.

Even from start, even when bud, Leaver moves further from Mama than Mama wants. Leaver digs deeper, Leaver argues when Mama says sleep. Leaver argues when Mama says soak. Then, one day, birds attack.

My new leaves curl inward at talk of birds.

Evil birds, Mama scents. *Birds dive down straight from sun, dig claws into stalk, pull seeds from fruit. Fruits broken open and bleeding. All those seeds. All gone.*

My sunhead shrinks down.

All those seeds, all dead. The sad from Mama is so thick. *But Leaver, he talks to evil birds.* We all breathe it in: disbelief, anger, outrage.

How does he talk, Mama?

He talks with vibrating leaves, pushing air. She scents disgust. Leaver is so low, so vulgar.

And then he abandons. I give him name: Leaver. And I have you beautiful, good children, my last seeds. You do not leave. You do not betray.

Leaver must go! Second sprays.

Send him back to bird friends. Third scents pure anger.

You tell him, Mama scents to me. *You are oldest, first seed.*

*

I finally scent Leaver at far edge of mamafield, past

where I have ever dug. I don't feel safe so far outcircle, but he's traveled alone for years. He's been so far outside we wouldn't even scent his death. And that's what he deserves.

The sun is full gone, so I move slowly, keep eyes closed. No need to waste energy for Leaver. I feel nightcat brush my stalk and I hold still until it's gone.

When I get close, Leaver scents before I can tell him Mama says leave.

I find field, he sprays. *Perfect beautiful field. Earth soft and deep without stones. Worms plenty.*

Why you talk to birds? I scent angry. *Birds are enemies.*

First I follow birds because I try to get seeds back for Mama.

Talk with vibrating leaves. I make sure to attach disgust to the scents.

How else?

Mama is right. Leaver is evil, like birds. Impossible to win argument with Leaver.

Birds don't understand, Leaver scents. *I vibrate leaves to push air. But birds don't talk back.*

You don't get seeds back, I scent.

I follow birds. I follow and follow. I travel over many hills. I grow weak, my stalk thin, no time for soaking. But I lose them, the birds. They fly too fast.

Birds are evil, I scent.

One day I find new bud, he scents. *New bud from seed. Seed dropped from birds. This new bud is my brother.*

Not possible. Now he lies. Brothers and sisters grow only with Mama.

But Leaver goes on. *His scent is true. He is new brother. I help him out of shade into full sun.*

Why new brother not here?

World is big, he scents. *Many fields.*

I don't understand. And then I do.

Other mamafields? I scent.

Little brother follows me. We find mamafield.

Other Mamas. I do not believe. There is only one Mama.

You know what else?

I don't want to know what else, but he goes on. *Anyone can make flower.*

It's too much. It's too wild, too strange. How can it be true? Everyone can flower? Seeds can travel far and become new buds without Mama.

You can flower, he scents.

No one flowers but Mama.

You could make flowers and collect pollen.

No.

But something inside me scents: yes.

You could make new buds.

No.

I think about little flowers. I think about the sweet smell of pollen and how it sticks to my leaves. I've dreamed of little flowers along my stalk, but I've never told Mama.

Leaver sniffs for my reply, but I don't have one.

My own flowers, I think. My own seeds, my own buds.

Leaver pulls his inward roots in, his outward roots out.

Where you go? I scent. I've forgotten for a moment, so strange are his stories.

I leave, he scents. *That's what Mama wants, true?*

It's night, I scent. But he keeps moving.

Wait.

He stops digging.

I talk to Mama. Maybe she wants to hear his crazy story. Mama will make sense of it. *I talk to Mama in morning.*

*

My eyes are open when the first good ray falls on world's edge. I want to go incircle, but still I wait until the grasses release their first scents.

I move in through my brothers and sisters, touching roots gently to wake.

What is it? Brother Fifth scents.

Does Leaver leave? scents Sister Fourth.

It's okay, I tell them. *I talk with Mama.*

Mama's eyes are open when I reach center. *Does Leaver leave?*

Soon, I scent.

That's what Leaver does, she scents. *Because Leaver not love Mama.*

Leaver says some things. He says he follows birds that day. He sees birds drop seeds. He sees new brother. From dropped seed.

How many seeds destroyed that day? She doesn't wait for my answer. *Fruit torn apart. Seeds drying and dying on mamafield.* I can barely understand the words for the pain attached.

It's okay, Mama. I scent comfort. *Leaver says new brother lives. Maybe other seeds live.*

No brothers and sisters grow without Mama.

Leaver says new brother finds new field.

No field without Mama.

I can go look. I don't tell her about other Mamas and how Leaver said anyone can flower. I think of traveling up and down the far hills. I think of tasting new soils and seeing new skies.

I'm thinking of all those new smells so I don't realize at first that Mama has not answered.

What, Mama?

My own bud. My first alive seed. She's spilling anger and hurt like a new bud. *You betray Mama.*

No, Mama. Not betray.

You vibrate leaves in air now too?

No, no, I scent. But really I mean yes. Because I'm thinking about following birds and seeing new mamafields. I feel ashamed. But I want her to understand. *Leaver says birds take fruit and drop seeds and seeds become new brothers and sisters.*

You believe Leaver.

Leaver has seen and smelled.

You defend Leaver. You defend birds. Birds kill my seeds. You don't love Mama.

I do love Mama. This is truth. I love Mama and I love my brothers and sisters.

If you love Mama you not go. You not believe Leaver.

The scents are deep with challenge. This is where I tell her I will never leave. That I will dig in the mamafield until I am old and all my leaves are long and wide and have soaked in all their sun and my roots can no longer dig. Until my stalk shrivels and my eyes shut fast. And then my brothers and sisters will push me into the shade trees and I will sink slowly back into the earth and all my pieces will become dirt.

But this is not what I want. I want to look over the far hills before I become soil. I want to see the rivers and the stone mountains and dig in the fields that Leaver has found. Maybe I even want to vibrate my leaves and try to make talk that birds can understand.

My hesitation speaks. I have not said please Mama forgive me. I have not said Mama I will never leave you.

Her hurt and anger hang thick around me.

I know what she'll spray at storytime. That I betray her, that I talk with birds. That evil Leaver tricks me to leave. And when the birds come again, she will say it is because me and Leaver told them to.

I want Mama to love me, I want her to say everything is okay. I want her to understand. I almost say I'll stay just so she'll stop the anger and hurt scents. Instead, I send roots out and pull myself away from Mama.

All my sisters and brothers give me path. They won't let their roots touch mine.

When I reach the edge of the circle I keep going. Leaver is further out than before, but he is still. He is waiting for me.

I move and move until I'm outcircle. All around me is wide unworked dirt. It's more difficult to furrow. But the soil is richer here. Even just a little ways out from mamafield there are plants I have never scented before.

I feel so lonely for Mama. But I can also feel strength inside me, new and free. Someday I'll find new mamafields. Someday I'll pollen. The sun is full out. My path is clear.

I feel the flowers inside me, waiting to bloom.

Looking Back

I watched Kira sleep. Soft breathing had turned to light snoring through the years, black hair to gray. She sleeps deepest in the quiet hours of early morning. There are no secrets when you've lived together thirty years in a nine hundred square foot house.

Almost no secrets.

The sun would rise soon, and I hadn't slept at all. Already the muddy light of the pre-dawn sky slipped through the bedroom blinds. I stared at Kira's tight gray curls against the ivory pillow and felt an unexpected tightening in my chest. I wanted to kiss her lightly on the foreheadlike in the old romances. One last goodbye, violins wailing in the background. But she might wake, and I couldn't chance it.

Russell followed when I left the bedroom, paws on carpet, silent as snow. A quick splash of water on my face from the bathroom sink, and I looked up briefly to the mirror, water dripping from my nose. Deep set eyes beneath dark eyebrows beneath white, bristled hair. Lines ran from the corners of my eyes all the way to below my chin. When had I become so old?

My pack was hidden in the hall closet, behind the vacuum cleaner that she used on Tuesdays and the old twelve-string I never played anymore.

Russell watched me expectantly while I changed into the clothes I had placed in the side pocket of the pack: thick jeans, a thermal undershirt, the flannel overshirt with the rip in the elbow that Kira had mended for me two times already.

I opened the door slowly, pausing each time the hinges protested, listening for sounds from the bedroom. Russell waited patiently through the slow process, head tilted quizzically, not making a sound. Smart, quiet, loyal Russell.

That *dog*, Kira would say, like it was a bad word, only half teasing. That *dog* is getting hair all over my couch. She never appreciated Russell. She would be glad that he was gone.

I stroked Russell's velvet head and ushered him out into the icy air.

Short, squat houses lined the street. Mine was only one in a long row of blank indistinguishable faces, windows like unblinking eyes.

Mine no longer. When the Tourists took me, I would be legally dead. The trust, the savings, my old truck, my cameras, everything would become hers. She would have the insurance as well. I had made sure she would be well taken care of.

The maples planted in the grassy border between the street and the sidewalk were growing too large for their confinement, their roots buckling the sidewalk. Soon they would be taken down for their crime of raising the uniform gray slabs.

The fog crept up from the river to lie across the road like a tired ghost.

I had never felt so alone. I had never felt so alive.

*

The Tourists came in gigantic ships. Golden and bullet shaped, like Buck Rogers of the Twenty-First Century, but bristling with antennae and sharp rigid fingers reaching radially outward.

The Tourists were human-sized, amorphous, soft-spoken. They used hard steel suits to protect themselves from our poisonous oxygen, our crushing sky.

They offered us a deal.

Come tour the universe with us, they said in Chinese, and then in every other human language. They laughed when the scientists asked how they knew our physiology, our languages. When you've toured a while, they said, you will see that there are far stranger beings than you. You are really quite ordinary.

We struggled to imagine the actual shape of their bodies, the form of their eyes and the color of their skin secreted within the solid oval suits. Endless speculation, a human specialty, dominated the TV and the radio.

What do we give up?

You give up your lives on Earth. When you Tour for fifty years, fifty thousand will pass on Earth. No one you know will be alive. Your descendants will have forgotten that you left.

What was in it for them? Nothing. They were Tourists. They wanted company for their journey.

A journey! Like I had yearned for when I was younger, wishing I could travel the world with just my camera and backpack. But that had never happened. Marriage had effectively trapped me in one city, with a mortgage and a job, and social obligations piling up like the unwanted bills on my desk.

"Do you believe them?" Kira asked one night, glued to the TV like everyone else around the world, as footage of the gold ships and steel suits played over and over.

"Yes," I answered.

On the screen a gold bullet furred with antennae and sensors slid up through a purpling sky. The first ship. Thousands of people set out to explore, to watch the birth of stars, to sail the huge, open, waiting universe. I had seen pictures: nebulae and swirling galaxies in an astonishing spectrum of colors, hues I could never seem to capture in my own photography. To step foot on the surface of planets in distant galaxies, plateaus overlooking unfathomable depths, gaseous atmospheres as deep and thick as a family secret. Exploration, enlightenment. A chance to glimpse the heavens.

My heart fluttered at the sight. *Set me free.*

Kira turned to me, as if she had heard.

"Why would anyone get on that ship and fly god knows where and leave everything they know behind?"

"Exploring is in our blood," I said. "That's why people came to America. That's why we still cross the North Pole and dive the ocean." The words were pathetically inadequate to describe the ecstasy of exploration, the thrill of an unknown destination. The pictures on the screen defied the ordinariness of our living room: mushroom brown furniture, throw rugs and framed crochet on the walls.

She used to understand. When we were young, we would plan trips together. Someday soon, we told each other, we'll see the Tibetan plateau, the Great Barrier Reef. Like love, the dream had faded with time.

"The people who leave will be bored within a week," she said. "And then they'll be stuck and unhappy and wishing they were home."

"For some people, I'm sure that's true."

She gave me an appraising look. I didn't dare say more. I watched the TV steadily.

*

The houses petered out altogether on the edge of Flagstaff, a half mile from the launch site. The first hint of light at the horizon tinged the clouds a muted yellow, a promise of gold. Already I could see the twisted spires of the shuttle, hands groping for the sky. It would launch at sunrise.

I hefted the pack higher on my back and quickened my pace. Russell padded beside me, claws clicking against asphalt, head low, tired already.

"Hang in there, old boy," I said.

He wheezed a little now, and he couldn't bend low to the ground to sniff out a trail or wiggle sideways like a Bendy-Stick, as he had when he was a puppy.

A long line of cars blocked the road.

Guards stood every ten feet along a perimeter of chain-link fence. I joined the line at the gate entrance.

In front of me was a solitary woman, stooped and gray-haired, carrying nothing. In front of her was a family of four, with ten suitcases on a cart, and a small black cat, meowling its displeasure. The two children were bright-eyed, curious, cranky. The cruise ship would be as big as the world they knew. Maybe bigger.

When I signed up for the journey, I told them what I would bring: my pack, my dog. The Tourists said there was plenty of food, that we would be comfortable. Still, some people wanted to bring their entire houses. Maybe they didn't really want to leave.

I took the little Pentax from my coat pocket: f-stop 22 for

the glistening golden shuttle beyond the fence. Its brightness dared the sun to rise and compete.

I hadn't brought a watch, but the rumble in my stomach told me I had missed breakfast. Kira would be up. I thought of her searching the house, at the slow realization transforming her face.

My throat tightened at the thought. She would be all right, I told myself. She had her friends, her sisters. They would help her find someone else. Someone settled, a Stayer, with no love of the stars, no sense of awe at the beauty of the universe, no unfulfilled need to explore and discover.

*

The ships were scattered across the globe: Africa, Siberia, Australia, Asia. These were the shuttles, the Tourists said, to take us to the bigger ship, the cruise ship, as big as the African continent. There would be room enough for farms and towns. We could organize governments and police forces if we wanted.

The world was split. The Stayers warned of deception. They said the Tourists wanted us for their own experiments, or maybe for fuel. Some said we would be pets, like the parrots the Spaniards took home from the Pan-Americas after spreading their diseases. We would be the talking birds in lonely golden cages on a conquistador's balcony. We would die of boredom.

The Deserters pointed out the incredible opportunity

offered by the Tourists. We, of all the generations before, had the chance to explore the universe. We would fulfill our true human potential, to reach the stars. Only one in a thousand said they would join the Tourists.

I couldn't understand why more people didn't want to go. People lived in an invisible, entangling web: Parents, children, lovers, jobs, houses. The Stayers lacked the strength to extricate themselves from their own lives.

*

The day of my decision, I had been in my darkroom. In the dim red light I watched the images emerge slowly from their chemical depths, photos from the outskirts of Flagstaff. Indistinct shapes became small houses with smaller yards, paper bags and empty bottles against chain-link fences, flattened and dying lawns. Houses too weary to lift tilting shutters, to hold onto chipped paint.

No one would buy them. I went to every gallery, every art show, every year. Kira said it was a waste of time. She was right.

From outside my small sanctuary, the sound of the television blared away as Kira got her nightly fix. What was the appeal? Eternally happy people with easily solvable problems. She had long ago stopped asking me to watch with her.

One month, the TV announcer droned. One month until the Tourists would leave. Make your decision now.

It made my whole body shake, thinking of how I would feel when they left. I imagined living out the rest of my tired days trapped beneath the Earth's thick atmosphere that blocked the universe from view. A whole life spent grabbing a free minute here and there to practice my photography, while Kira numbed herself a room and a universe away.

I picked up a photograph using a pair of metal tongs, and there it was in the foreground: a single dandelion, poking impossibly through the tiniest of cracks in the sidewalk, the night's condensation wet and glistening on its hopeful leaves and bulbous head.

Suddenly, the decision was easy.

I knew in that moment that I could not turn down the chance to fly. My destiny was written. I would go on the next ship. I would not look back.

*

A woman in an orange safety vest, skin red from exposure, checked my ID against her list. I set my pack on the ground and waited.

The wind rattled the chain-link fence. I could hear the murmuring of those in line behind me, the hushed, tense tones.

Finally, the guard smiled at me, blue eyes reflecting the first light of dawn, and nodded me through.

I walked onward.

Sparse grass crunched beneath my boots. The sun loitered just above the horizon, a simmering orange-red globe. The shuttle towered above.

I walked into its shadow, and the air grew chilly.

At the base of the shuttle was a wide ramp leading up into its interior. I walked up, and found myself in a circular room, where a dozen other Deserters waited quietly. I held my pack tight against my chest with one hand, my other on Russell's collar. A door slid shut, and I felt myself rising. An elevator.

A moment later, the door opened again, and we squeezed out into a large room filled with seats. The walls and floors were brushed copper, the seats wide and soft, better than First Class. This would be our home for the ten-hour journey to the cruise ship.

One entire wall was a window. I walked over to it, Russell beside me.

To the left and right were other viewrooms, other faces pressed against the hard transparent surfaces, curving out of view around the ship.

Below I saw the ramp into the ship, and further on, the chain-link fence with the line of Deserters. The line was shorter now. The Stayers huddled behind, mouths opening and closing in a silent chant. Too late.

Already I could feel a vibration through my feet, a rumbling promising a roar. The shuttle would launch on schedule.

*

Once I had made the decision, the rest was easy.

I signed up in the police station in downtown Flagstaff one afternoon after work. Another man stood at the counter. I tried to give him a friendly smile, but he wouldn't meet my eye. Going on the Journey was nothing to be ashamed of.

The officer behind the counter took my thumbprint, my picture.

I never doubted they would let me go. They made us register to keep track of who left, and to weed out the crazy people, the criminals. But the ones who truly wanted to journey were the most sane people of all.

When I pulled up at home later, Kira was in the front yard. She had spread a blanket on the dirt, and was tugging at the weeds surrounding the base of the small mandarin orange tree she had planted the previous spring.

Her shoulders tensed when I approached, though she didn't turn to look at me.

"It died," she said.

It took me a moment to realize she was talking about the tree. I looked at the thin, peeling branches of the tree, at the gray buds that had died almost as soon as they appeared.

I had told her the tree wouldn't last through our harsh winter, but Kira had insisted, saying that the mandarin is especially cold-hearty.

Kira held a Kleenex to her nose. Was she actually crying at the death of a plant?

When I was younger I might have comforted her. I might have gone out to buy her another tree, knowing all along that it was a futile mission.

I gazed upwards, where the Tourists' ship was visible as a single bright point of light in the sky. Even in midday it was easy to pick out. Soon, I would be up there.

"I'm sorry, Kira," I said. I turned and went into the house to find my pack.

*

We were lifting, as gentle as a balloon at sunrise, straight up toward the quiet black of space. I set my pack at my feet so I could move closer to the window. Already the ground was five hundred feet below, the trees like bits of steel wool scattered across the pale ground.

It was silent within, the whisper of fabric against fabric, an occasional low cough. The young man to my left in fatigues and a thick wool coat pressed his nose to the window, his hands on either side.

The sun's rays streaked the ground in long red arrows. It was so beautiful from above.

The girl next to me held on to her mother's hand and looked up at her with the sudden, desperate realization of a child. "We'll never see our house again?"

The mother placed a hand on her shoulder and pulled her close. "I don't think so."

We'll see much better things, I wanted to say. But there would be time to talk. There would be years and years to talk.

Russell whined.

I opened the top of the pack to take out his breakfast, and there, below the Tupperware of kibble, was a brown paper bag.

I hadn't packed it.

I withdrew it slowly. The surface was lined and worn from reuse, just like the lunch bags Kira packed for me when I went on shoots.

Inside was a small container of applesauce, a plastic bag with a sandwich. Deviled egg, my favorite. I closed the bag again, pressed it to my chest. Thirty years and I thought I had known her. How could she have slept last night, knowing I was leaving? I closed my eyes. I imagined her slipping beneath the comforter, whispering a soft goodnight, knowing her husband would be gone when she woke in the morning.

I felt a tugging on my coat and opened my eyes.

The little girl was pulling on my jacket hem.

"What will you miss the most?" she said. Her mother smiled apologetically at me.

The blues and greens and grays were blurring below, the houses merging into long rows of tan against the darker roads. The headlights of the cars parked outside the site gate were a solid, glowing line, leading all the way back to town.

What would I miss?

The lightning in the plains, so bright the whole sky sizzles into white hot life for an instant, and then goes absolutely black; driving at night in the summer with the window rolled down all the way and the warm rain against my face and the wipers zwipp-zwipping in tune to Nina Simone. The throaty warble of a red-winged blackbird in the cattails. The way the fog creeps through the pines by the Colorado river on a cold January morning. The hot, dry smell of the desert. A packed lunch.

How long had she known? The possibilities exploded outward, like the fast-motion film of a flowering orchid, petaled layers concealing velvety depths.

The little girl was staring up at me expectantly.

"Deviled egg," I told her.

She nodded solemnly, satisfied with my answer.

Below, the cities and lakes shrunk to silver-streaked pebbles. I placed a hand on the cold transparent surface before me, looking back.

Big Brave Rita

Rita woke to a bright light coming through her curtains. She sat up and looked out her window. Mama and Papa and Oma were standing outside with the people from town. The town truck rumbled, its lights on an inky object in the road.

She hugged her blankie around her shoulders and got out of bed. The smell of lavender spilled over her when she opened the front door. Mama said it hadn't always smelled like that at night. Just since the Blobbies came.

She walked over to the group, squeezed through until she was just behind Oma. She could barely see the thing through everyone's legs, but she was pretty sure it was a Blobbie. She had seen Blobbies through the pain-fence. It had that black rubbery skin and the long twitching snout. Except this one's snout was not twitching. It looked dead, like the antelope she had seen once at the side of the road, big and solid and not moving.

"Someone turn off that damn engine," Jody said. "It's wasting gas."

"What are you doing here?" That was Papa's voice.

Everyone turned to look at Rita.

"Where are your shoes?" Mama said.

Oma took Rita's hand and led her back to the house.

"Is it dead?" Rita said.

"We can't tell," Oma said.

"How come?"

"Blobbies are very different from us. We don't even know if they breathe like us."

Rita thought about that for a moment. Everyone talked about the Blobbies all the time, but no one seemed to know anything about them. "How else would it breathe?"

Oma helped Rita into bed and tucked the blankie under her chin. "Well, maybe it breathes through gills, like a fish. Or maybe it doesn't need to breathe at all. How about a story?"

Oma took out the book of Big Brave Rita. Rita loved the lumpy pages. Opa had made the book for her before he went to heaven, made the paper and the colors all himself from the plants and rocks. She tried not to open it too often because Oma said the colors would fade a little bit each time the sun touched the paper.

Oma read the story out loud, even though Rita knew the

story by heart. When the Blobbies first came, Big Brave Rita led an army of people and animals across the land. But the Blobbies fought back and built the pain-fence. They put all the people behind the pain-fence and took over the cities and stunk up the world with their lavender smell. Papa said Rita would be like Big Brave Rita when she grew up, and that's why they named her Rita. She and her friends would figure out how to take down the pain-fence and everyone would be free again like in the stories of the time before when everyone could get whatever they wanted from the stores, like bananas and antibiotics, and everyone could go wherever they wanted all the time, even to the far away land of Ohio.

*

In the morning, Rita heard cries coming from the cellar.

"Who is crying?" Rita said.

Mama put a bowl of oatmeal in front of Rita. "Hush," she said. "No one is crying."

"But I can hear it."

It was a strange sort of crying. A whining, snuffling sort of crying, like the sound the dogs made sometimes when they were excited about dinnertime. But it was definitely crying.

Papa came upstairs with two other men. His shirt was spotted with black ink. He washed his hands in the water bucket by the sink. In the sunlight the ink looked colorful, like the oil spots on the road from the town truck.

"Bastard won't talk," he said.

"Watch your language," Mama said with a glance at Rita.

"Go to your room, Rita," Papa said. "We have to discuss something."

"But I want to see the Blobbie," she said.

Papa looked at her, and his eyes were very wide and a little sad. "Maybe later," he said. Rita was familiar with 'maybe'. Maybe meant never.

Rita got up and went to her room, where she could hear everything perfectly well.

"It's been hurt," Mama said. "And it could be young. Maybe it hasn't learned to talk yet."

"It can talk. It just doesn't want to."

"What do you think it was doing inside the compound?"

"Who the hell cares? It's ours now."

Dishes clinked together. Mama always saved them up until she got a fresh bucket of water.

"The others are going to come looking for it," Mama said. When Papa's voice got louder, Mama's always got softer.

"Think about this, Kailee. This is the opportunity we've been waiting for. We get it to tell us how the fence works, then we disable that damn fence, get across to the other compounds. We organize. We fight back. We have to do this now. This may be the only chance we ever have to get out of here!"

Rita looked out her window at the cracked road and the way the air shimmered in hazy waves above the shiny spots. Oma said all the roads used to be super smooth, not cracked and lumpy like they were now, and they used to run everywhere, to places with green grass all year round or deep blue lakes. Oma said there used to be a town called Vegas not far away that had high, high buildings and giant lights even at night and water fountains everywhere even though it was the middle of the desert. Now the road only went into town in one direction and ended at the pain-fence in the other direction. Everywhere inside the fence was just reddish-brown dirt and rocks and low bushes with thorns that only the goats could eat. Rita's family lived on the edge of town, next to the gardens and the goats and chicken pens. The pain-fence was a silver web going half way up the sky, just past the chickens.

Rita wondered if the Blobbie went under the fence or just through it. Oma said the Blobbies didn't feel pain when they went through the fence. She wondered if the Blobbie had come to tell them how to take down the pain-fence, like Papa thought. Or maybe it had just come to visit and say hello.

*

"Maybe the Blobbie is sad," Rita said when Oma came to read her a story that night.

"Maybe it is." Oma looked sad, too.

"Papa said it is evil and all Blobbies go to hell."

"Rita, you remember when Joshua from town got in trouble because he had a big fight with his wife?"

"Yes." Papa said Joshua was a bad man. Joshua's wife had a big bruise on her cheek for two weeks.

"But then how he saved that puppy from the fence?"

Rita nodded. Joshua had stood next to the pain-fence and pulled the puppy out, even though it made him hurt all over and have nightmares for a long time after.

"Well, maybe the Blobbies are like Joshua. Maybe they can do both bad and good things."

Rita thought about the Blobbie in the cellar, and wondered if it had ever saved a puppy from the pain-fence. No one had ever seen dogs on the other side of the fence. Just big shiny metal houses and Blobbies racing around in their floating cars and sometimes the big machines that dug into the ground and burped lavender-smelling gas.

*

The Blobbies came looking the next morning. They came in their floating cars that looked like rocks that sparkled in places. Hematite, Oma called it. She had studied rocks in college. A college was a place where a bunch of people sat and listened to one person talk and explain about rocks.

Everyone went to meet the Blobbies because they said "Gather!" in their big booming fake-voice.

Rita stood on the edge of the crowd, but she couldn't understand what the Blobbies were saying. Everyone said they were so smart, but they didn't speak English very well. Maybe they were both smart and not-smart, like they were good and not-good at the same time.

Rita snuck away and ran back to the house. First she went

to her room and got her checkers board, then she went down to the cellar. The door wasn't locked. There was a heavy cross beam, but Papa always said she was strong for her size. She lifted it and pushed the door open.

It smelled like flowers that had been on the kitchen table too long and needed to have their water changed. And a little like the outhouse.

There was just enough light from the cracks in the walls.

The Blobbie was really big. A big, quivering black blob.

"Hello," Rita said.

Its long snout poked out from the rubbery skin. Its snout had red and black blotches on it. Oma had said that's where it smelled and saw and spoke, that it was very sensitive. All its little arms and legs were wrapped in rope, even its tiny little front pincher arms, and its body was tied to the main pillar under the house.

The snout sniffed the air just like a mouse nose, twitching this way and that.

Rita took the checkers board from under her arm and set it in front of the Blobbie.

"My Oma made this for me," she said. "She does wood working."

She explained the rules, just like Oma had taught her.

"Jump, jump, jump." She said, showing the Blobbie with the black checker jumping over the red checker.

She set up the board again.

The Blobbie hesitated, then its snout nudged a red

checker on the board.

"Good move," Rita said.

She won the first game, but then she felt sorry for the Blobbie, with all its limbs tied up like that, and she let it win the second game. It won the third all on its own.

"You're a fast learner," she said. She wished she could untie it, but she knew that would make Papa mad.

She heard shouts from outside. The Blobbie started to quiver. "Don't cry," Rita said. "I'll come back." She quickly put all the pieces back in the drawstring bag and tucked the board under her arm. She put the crossbeam back across the door and ran up the stairs just in time.

Papa and a crowd were standing in front of the house.

"They don't mean it," Jody from town said. She held a rifle across her shoulders. With the sun setting all red and orange behind her and her hat making a black shadow across her face, she looked like Big Brave Rita from the book. But Big Brave Rita helped the animals, and Jody never even noticed the animals.

"They mean it," her Papa said. "We have to make a decision."

"We have to fight," Jody said. "Once we get the information we need."

The other people were talking about how they would make spears and bows and arrows and long knives from scrap metal, and how once they overthrew the Blobbies they would be able to travel again and start factories and fix the roads and have bathtubs filled with hot water.

"The first thing I'll do is find some seeds and grow a coffee plant," someone said. Everyone sighed. Whenever anyone said anything about coffee, everyone else sighed.

"Don't be an idiot," Jody said. "Coffee wouldn't grow here. Now quiet down. We need to make a decision."

"Not here," Papa said. "They're probably watching us right now."

Everyone left for Jody's house.

Rita ran into the house and got her Big Brave Rita book. She ran back down to the cellar.

"We can read this here because we're not in the direct sun," Rita said. "The sun makes the colors go away."

She opened it for the Blobbie, who snuffled its trunk over the pages, but was careful not to get any black ink on the pages.

The Blobbie started huffing and snuffling.

"Don't cry," Rita said. "It's not a sad story. See how Big Brave Rita saves all the animals? I'm named after her."

But the Blobbie wouldn't stop snuffling. Ink oozed from its skin.

Rita ran upstairs and got the gauze from the bathroom.

She tried to put the gauze over the place where the black oil came out of the Blobbie, but it squirmed and squirmed and the gauze just turned black and soggy.

*

It was nighttime and Rita was asleep, but Papa came into her room and made her wake up.

The moon made enough light that she could see he was holding a soggy piece of gauze and he was very mad.

"Rita, did you do this?"

Rita tried not to squirm. "It was hurt," she said.

"I told you not to go down there."

No, he hadn't. Not really. She held her head up defiantly. "We played checkers."

Papa squeezed the gauze inside his hand. She could see black ink leaking between his knuckles. "Did it talk to you?"

She shook her head. "It was crying."

Papa picked up her checkers game and tucked it under his arm. He took her by the hand and led her out of the room. Mama and Oma were in the kitchen. They both stood up when Papa led Rita out the back door.

"What are you doing, George?" Oma said.

Papa didn't listen. He led Rita outside and downstairs to the cellar.

They stood inside the door until their eyes adjusted.

Papa dragged Rita over to the Blobbie. The Blobbie quivered and shrank back.

"Talk," Papa said. Rita wasn't sure if he was talking to the Blobbie or to her. Or maybe both. The Blobbie quivered and quivered.

Papa held the checker board over his head. Then he hit the Blobbie. The Blobbie's skin cracked and black ink came out. Its snout tried to disappear, but Papa's hand snaked out and grabbed the snout.

He held up the board again.

"No, Papa!" Rita said. She tried to catch Papa's hand. Then she saw Oma was there, too, and Oma was holding Papa's other arm and keeping him from hitting the Blobbie.

"What the hell!" Papa said. Rita had never heard him so loud before.

There was a loud crash from outside, then lots of voices. Mama shouted into the cellar. "George, the Blobbies are here! Come quick!"

But Papa never had a chance to come quick. The Blobbies were suddenly there in the cellar, a lot of them, and they barely fit. They held a really bright light and Rita couldn't see anything. She was pushed back into the corner by all the rubbery bodies. Where was Oma? Where was Papa?

Then the Blobbies moved a little and Rita could see Papa held between two Blobbies with a silvery net. Her Blobbie, the bleeding Blobbie, was free and he was waving all his little arms and snuffling some more.

The biggest Blobbie said, "Child for child," in that funny fake-voice, like the truck wheels on gravel.

"No!" Papa said. He squirmed against the silvery net.

"No!" Oma squeezed through the Blobbies and knelt next to Rita and held her very tight.

"No," another voice said. It was the bleeding Blobbie. Its voice was gravelly, too.

"Child for child," the big Blobbie said again, and reached out its trunk for Rita.

Then there was a loud bang. Rita covered her ears, and one of the Blobbies screamed in a high-pitched gurgly scream. Suddenly everyone was moving all at once and Rita was being pulled away from Oma. Her Blobbie friend was trying to stand between Big Blobbie and Rita, and then there was another loud bang and Big Blobbie turned and snorted through its trunk and another silver net flew through the air. Big Blobbie pulled on a silver string and Jody bounced down the cellar stairs in the net. Her rifle clanked on the stone steps next to her.

Big Blobbie picked up the rifle and broke it in half with three of its pincher-limbs.

Then for a moment everyone was still and all Rita could hear was a high-pitched ringing. Everyone was looking down and covering their ears, so Rita looked down too and saw Oma lying on the cellar floor taking a nap.

"You shot her," someone said.

"It was an accident," Jody said, trying to push out of the net.

Rita knelt next to Oma. "Wake up, Oma. It's okay now. The Blobbies broke the rifle." Oma would be glad. She always said that rifle would lead to no good. She tugged on Oma's hand. But Oma did not move.

Rita's ears hurt, and maybe that's why the tears were coming out of her eyes. She put her head on Oma's shoulder.

"Wake up, Oma," she said. "Please wake up."

"God, no. No!" That was Papa, still squirming in his own net. "You goddamn bastards!"

Little Blobbie started snorting through its trunk again and again and tugging on Big Blobbie's long arms. The other Blobbies were still.

Finally, Big Blobbie wrapped one of its long arms around Little Blobbie. Rita saw that they were going to take Little Blobbie away. Its snout twitched at Rita, and then the whole group of Blobbies squeezed up the cellar stairs and got into their hematite cars and flew up into the air. Rita could see up the cellar stairs that the dirt and pebbles flew up and swirled around and around and all the people from town were staring up and not even noticing the dust landing in their hair and on their faces.

After the Blobbies left it was dark again. Rita heard someone crying and realized it was Papa. She had never heard Papa cry before. He sounded like the Blobbie, snuffling and snorting and making strange squeaking noises.

Mama knelt by him and cut the silvery net with a kitchen knife. He sat up and put his head in his hands. Then Mama came to Rita and hugged her tight and rocked back and forth a little.

Rita looked over Mama's shoulder at Oma, still lying on the floor.

"Will Oma wake up?" Rita asked.

"Shush," Mama said.

The people from town came down the stairs and set Jody free from her silvery net. Soon Jody left with the broken pieces of her rifle, but lots of people were still in the cellar and they were talking in whispers and milling around like after church. Some were trying to talk to Papa but he didn't notice.

"It's time for bed," Mama said.

"Wait," Rita said. She picked up the checkerboard and collected the checkers that were all over the floor and put them back in their drawstring bag. No one said anything while she picked them up. She put them in Oma's hands.

"She doesn't understand," someone said.

But Rita did understand. She knew that Oma would want to play checkers in Heaven with Opa.

And she knew that Oma would never read her bedtime stories again.

Right then and there Rita decided she never wanted to hear the story of Big Brave Rita ever again. And not just because Oma couldn't read it to her anymore. She didn't want to be like Big Brave Rita, no matter what Papa said.

When she got older, she would make up her own story, and it wouldn't have Big Brave Rita in it, or Jody, or any rifles either. And it wouldn't have coffee, because she didn't know what that was, or bananas or hot running water. But it would have the pain-fence and her Blobbie friend, and the smell of lavender, because those were the things she knew. And it would have the goats and chickens and the green bean patch and Oma, because those were the things she loved.

Maps to God

Here's the thing about my mother: she's been fading out for years. These days I can't understand her unless the electromagnetic fields line up just so.

Just yesterday evening at dinner she tuned in and out as I twisted the fork in my hand: "—Dr. Franklin—staff is excellent—not enough—"

I finally got the angle just right: "Herb, I bought the medication."

Fortunately, my dad is on my frequency, so I don't need utensils to hear him. "We already discussed this, Joan," he said.

Tum-ticka tum. I ain't no holla-back girl. That's the other thing about my frequency—it's tuned to pick up secret signals from a Gnostic sect hidden deep in the Sahara. Or possibly Nevada. They send me messages coded in pop songs.

My mother's mouth opened and closed but the electromagnetic wind must have shifted because I could no longer hear her. My father shook his head at what she said. The setting sun angled through the kitchen window and bloodied the white tablecloth between my parents. I heard the clank of silverware and the ever-present hum of background radiation like a perpetual motion refrigerator.

I shifted so that the sprig of dogwood blossom in the table vase blocked my view of my mother and applied my fork to dinner. I segregated the little rosemary spears from the potatoes. It was a long job, but necessary; my mother might have applied truth-serum to the tips of the spears. She was always trying to trip me up, get me to tell her my plans.

"No," my father said. "Remember what happened last time?"

I always loved the one-sided conversation. It was a puzzle.

"Come on, Joan. Leave her alone."

I looked up. My mother had obviously just addressed me; her face was expectant.

"She wants to know what you're working on now," my father said.

"It's proprietary," I said. *Tum-ticka-tum.*

I didn't expect my mother to understand. Even though I'm

still a teenager she knows I could be the next Einstein, and it scares her. Some people are afraid of genius.

I've been ostracized by the scientific community for years. The National Academy of Sciences has never answered any of my letters. They just don't understand the importance of my work. They don't understand that I could have made teleportation work if I just had the right tools. At least the Gnostics believe in me.

This time I'm working on something big. I mean really big. It's a map to God, and it will change everything.

*

After dinner my father helped me in the lab.

"Wire cutters!" I sang.

"Wire cutters." My father passed me the red-handled ones.

My music swelled. *Ticka-ticka-tum-TICKA. We are THE CHAMPIONS.* It's so sad that he can't hear it. My father believes in me even though he doesn't understand the physics behind my work.

"Tape!"

"We're out."

"Jesus Christ!" I couldn't help myself. "We're so close!"

"How does this machine work?" he asked.

"It's difficult to pinpoint," I answered.

A map to God is a paradox: every step of the journey is a piece of understanding, which leads you further from God.

Every step closer is also a step further away.

My dad looked up from the machine. My mother stood in the doorway to my laboratory, hands on her hips, frowning.

I didn't used to have a lab in the basement.

Last year when I was sixteen my mother tried to help with my invisibility machine even though she didn't have the scientific background and I didn't need her help. That day she sat down next to me while I was working on the control box, picked up a capacitor, and put it in completely the wrong place.

I took her capacitor out.

How was that helping, I ask you. It wasn't.

She said something.

She reached in to the control box and took one of mine out. That was really not helping. I slapped her hand away.

She stood up and the control box overturned. And it had been almost done! I pounded the capacitors on the floor. Anger in my fists, anger in my fingers.

My mother's mouth moved and her face turned red. She stood up and tripped over the power supply cables which scavenged left-over kinetic energy from my sneakers.

I felt the vibration of her voice in my teeth, even though I couldn't hear her.

Later that day my dad helped me cart all my lab equipment downstairs. He said I had to work in the basement from then on.

We set up my equipment in the east side of the basement.

On the other side was the washing machine, and in the middle was a piece of orange carpet and a couch.

My dad stood up, knees creaking. "Good luck with your machine."

I continued on with the wires. Red to black. Black to red. *Tum-ticka-tum.* I could do this without duct tape.

*

When I went upstairs to get some water my mother trapped me in a transition point. That's the thing about doorways, certain pathways, anything that helps you move from one place to another. Most people move through easily, don't even notice them. I get stuck in them, and my mother takes advantage of that.

She stepped in front of me as I was trying to get from the living room into the kitchen. I tried to move but I was held tight by the transition force, a giant hand on my shoulder.

She held up an orange bottle with typed words on the side. What poison had she concocted for me now?

She twisted open the lid. Small white pills spilled into her hand.

She smiled and held out her hand.

They were such tiny pills. How could she think that anything so small could affect me in any way? It struck me as funny, and I began to laugh.

My mother shoveled the pills back into the bottle, her lips pressed tight. Several dropped onto the floor, rolled this way and that. One rolled through the doorway and ended my paralysis. I followed the pill through the doorway.

Dum. Dum. Dum. Another one bites the dust.

My father sat in the living room reading a paper. My mother must have said something to him because he said, without looking up. "I won't make her take anything she doesn't want to."

My mother bent to gather up the pills, hands shaking. One had escaped. It lay in the crack between where the kitchen tiles ended and the living room carpet began. It was stuck in a transition. I knew what that was like. I felt a sudden kinship with the little pill.

I put my foot over it, pressed it further into the crack to keep it safe from my mother's enormous groping hands.

"Do not be afraid, little one," I whispered. I hummed softly to it. *Hum. Hum. Hum.*

My mother walked away. Her back was very straight.

I would come back later and rescue the pill. I had a moment of inspiration: the pill was vitally important for my machine.

*

When I was young I could still hear my mother pretty well. One day when I was nine she lured me to the front of the house with the promise of a trip to the science museum.

She stood by the front door in a suit. Green light from the stained-glass inset spilled around her like a sick halo.

"Are you finally ready?" she said.

She had only worn that suit once before to uncle Mark's wedding. She would never wear it to the museum.

I would have run except that she had already trapped me in the transition point of the hallway. I sat down on the floor. I held my backpack over my head. I thought maybe all the metal in there would shield me.

"Herb!"

My dad came back in, carrying the car keys. He didn't look at me.

"We're already late," my mother said.

He tried to lift me up by my arms. The backpack fell open, and all my lab supplies skittered here and there: antennae, transducer coils, power supplies.

"Jesus Christ," my mother said. "What is all that junk?"

My dad squatted next to me and helped me gather the equipment.

"Dr. Franklin won't wait forever," my mother said. "Just leave it."

"No!" I said.

"I don't know what good Dr. Franklin is going to do anyway," my father said.

I hugged the transceivers to my chest.

"Forget it," my mother said. "Just forget it." She slammed the front door on her way out.

That's when I knew she would never understand me.

*

Midnight. Alone in the basement. It was my habit to work late into the night, long after my parents had gone to sleep. That's when I did my best thinking, when the signals from the Gnostics got through loud and clear. *Love is a battlefield.*

I kept thinking of that little pill upstairs, trapped in the gritty boundary between tile and carpet. Carpet fuzz to the west, unyielding tile to the east.

I crept upstairs and with a plastic knife, freed the renegade pill from its prison. The basement door frame gave us a bit of a problem, but eventually the pill and I slid through sideways, my back scraping against the door jam, and we made it back to my machine.

The machine was almost ready.

The metal had to be carefully arranged so that the magnetic field lines of the earth (albeit small) would coincide with the induced field lines of the metal. The current I got from a dead light bulb. Transitions are fuzzy; there is a little bit of death in life, and a bit of life in death.

A special aluminum-tipped wedge served as a conduit, coaxing out the last bit of power from the bulb. Four spherical transceivers, a prism to cut and spread the energy of photons, a fine mesh to capture and distil the mystery that is God.

Here's the key to the machine: God is in the transitions. God is the moment just passed. The instant you think you've put your finger on it, it has slipped into the past. God is the moment about to come. It is always just out of reach.

I only had to capture a moment, hold it still for an instant.

I washed the courageous pill with the light from the prism. I placed it first in the tray of the machine so that it would soak up the precisely aligned magnetic fields, and then into my mouth, where in four hours it would bring me face to face with God.

*

I woke in the morning on the little strip of carpet next to the basement couch. Light shone through the dusty half-windows which looked out past the garbage cans onto the front lawn.

My machine stood on an upside-down plastic folding chair. Twine wound through the legs, creating a see-through basket. Aluminum foil balls adorned the feet. A prism hung from a key chain attached to a dead light bulb.

I stood and pushed the prism. As it swung, the colors of the rainbow washed over the litter on the floor: red sheaths of plastic from stripped wires, bolts and nuts and nails and screws. My equipment. My laboratory. My sad machine.

"No," I said. It no longer looked like a machine, like a key to anything.

And the Gnostics—they had deserted me. I could hear morning jays calling to each other. I could hear a bus grinding the pavement outside, but I could not hear my music. My head was empty as a carved-out pumpkin.

I ran to the stairs, up the stairs, to the doorway, through the doorway. I was strangely unhindered by transitions.

Failure, failure. My machine had not worked.

I went to the front door and opened it. Outside, dandelions sagged over the front stoop, dew clinging to their leaves. There was a bus stop directly in front of our walk. I remembered waiting there sometimes, holding my mother's hand. I remembered riding the bus downtown with her to the science museum, an hour away. I remembered my mother's bright blue cardigan and her singing softly to me in time with our steps up the wide cool stairs of the museum, and the giant concrete lion out front.

"You're up early."

I turned. My mother stood behind me in a ratty bathrobe. Her hair was not in place.

"Are you going out," she said in a flat tone, not really a question. She moved away, as if she did not expect a reply. My mother was a stooped and graying woman. The years were written in liver spots on her arms, in the way her mouth turned down, afraid to smile. When had my mother become an old woman?

I blinked, swiveled my head this way and that, trying to find my frequency. Where had my music gone?

"Something's wrong with my head," I said.

My mother stopped. She turned and stared at me.

I knew in that instant that I would never forget the way my mother looked that morning. Her slumped shoulders, her lined face, time pivoting around us like a top dancing on its point, slowing, taunting, primed to topple.

And then, strangely, my mother began to cry.

Nothing. Only a whisper, but it was there. The Gnostics! They were coming through. I tested the doorway, felt a hint of resistance. Relief flooded through me. *Tik-tik.* The faintest brush of beat, like a grasshopper's legs preparing for the night.

"Have you talked to your father this morning?" my mother said. The last few words were so soft I could barely hear them. And then she said, "I thought—missed—but look."

"I'm going back downstairs," I said.

My mother wiped her eyes. She might have said something else.

Nothing's gonna change my world. I hurried through the hallway arch and through the basement door before the transition force could lay its clammy hands on me.

Ticka-ticka-tik. By the time I reached my machine, the music gurgled through my veins once more.

I surveyed the machine. The prism was at the wrong angle. The magnetic fields did not align.

The Gnostics had taught me that inside each person is the spark of the divine, and that it is just as real as the soup of the physical universe in which we swim, live and die.

But I think they are wrong. The divine spark is not inside or outside, but somewhere in between. God is not the attainment of knowledge, but the attempt at apprehension. God is in the cracks; God is everything we can't quite reach, everything we can't control. In the border between sanity and insanity. In every imagined story ending.

I began to think: Maybe it was impossible to capture a transition, but every time we go through one a piece of God sticks to us like lint on a sweater.

There are many maps to God.

This is one of them.

Looking for Friendship, Maybe More

003.19:23:12 Are U my Soulmate?
We shared a drink on High-Earth Orbit Station, then I find myself tied up in a space alien costume in that smelly zero-g commode. Anyway, I had a great time. Ping me.
~Helpless Romantic

003.19:35:00 Just One Night
I am a scientist (specialty: alien species) on leave at the Station for twenty-four hours. I can give you the most amazing experience ever. Also, I pay well. Self-holo attached.
=Research Scientist=

003.19:56:01 <u>Call to Arms!</u>
Fellow Station residents: The D'ohrahd are here to subjugate the human race! High-Earth Station is only their first conquest!! Earth will be next!! Stop them now!!! Join us at the protest at the D'ohrahd Welcoming tonight!!!!
-HumanOnly-
Live FREE or DIE A SLAVE!

003.20:10:55 Re: Just One Night
dear research scientist
i am available for your amazing experience...do u have any special requirements? rates attached...
--can-do
ps...love your hunky holo...

003.20:26:01: Call to Arms!
Hey everyone, a Protest sounds fun! Will there be dancing?
~Helpless Romantic

003.20:42:30 Seeking...
...a ride off this miserable station. Took a leave off planet. Did a little gambling. Next thing I know I'm stripped of bioware and penniless in high earth orbit. Will do anything in exchange for ticket back to earth. Anything. Please help.
-Penniless

003.21:03:12 Hire Me
I am a fix-it-all kind of guy. Space elevators, pods, implants. Nano. Good rates. References.

HandyMan
I can fix anything

-High Earth Orbit (HEO) Station Public Announcement-
HEO Board Administration apologizes for the interruption in service between 003:22:00 and 004:06:30. During the D'ohrahd Welcoming, several EM bombs were launched, resulting in the disruption of all electronic signals at the station.

004.07:27:20 Re:Re: Call to Arms!
Nice job, HumanOnly. You succeeded in sabotaging your own race. Next time see me about properly working equipment.

            HandyMan
      I can fix anything

004.07:52:20 Re:Re: Just One Night
research scientist
u weren't joking! that ring on your thing...u know what i'm talking about...will do that again anytime...in fact, accidentally took the ring...hope you don't mind that i used it again later...
-can-do

004.08:16:01 Re:Re:Re: Just One Night
Can-Do:
You must be mistaken. I still have the ring. But I'm happy to meet again before I leave.
=Research Scientist=

004.08:34:50 Re:Re:Re: Call to Arms!
humanOnly
i would be willing to role play as a d'ohrahd...i have the costume, very realistic...skinfeed works with almost all

bioware...
-can-do

004.08:35:50 Re:Re:Re:Re: Call to Arms!
Can-Do: you are not taking this seriously! The D'ohrahd are
here to kill us all and take over Earth!!
-HumanOnly-
Live FREE or DIE A SLAVE!

004.08:45:40 Re:Re:Re:Re:Re: Call to Arms!
Hey Can-Do, I'm interested in that costume. When&where?
~Helpless Romantic

004.08:47:40 Re:Re:Re:Re:Re:Re: Call to Arms!
Don't do it, Helpless! Do not betray your race!!
-HumanOnly-
Live FREE or DIE A SLAVE!

004.09:02:50 Re: Seeking...
Can-Do, you Just Did. No longer want a ride off-station. Love
it here. That ring. Even without biofeed. Wow. Thanks.
-Penniless

004.09:25:46 Re: Hire Me
handyman
i have a few things you could fix...what kind of uniform do
you wear?
-can-do

004.09:35:40 All Tied Up
Hey Can-Do: Last night we took a naked pod ride under the
stars and danced in zero-g. Would love to do it again.

Anytime. Ping me.
-Helpless
PS You left your ring.

004.09:42:51 Re: All Tied Up
helpless
i still have my ring...thanks for checking...happy to meet again...
-can-do

004.09:54:11 Re:Re: Seeking...
Actually I have the ring. And in fact, for some reason I have two rings now. Anyone want one back?
-Penniless

004.10:14:18 Re:Re:Re:Re:Re:Re:Re: Call to Arms!
Hey Can-Do: I had no idea it could be like that. However, I think there might be something caught in one of my orifices. I might not be able to meet you again for a while.
~Helpless Romantic

004.10:15:04 Re:Re: Hire Me
Hey Handyman, I just saw your post. Maybe you can help me out with an implant problem. Actually, not exactly an implant. As long as you are discreet. Need help soon.
~Helpless Romantic

004.10:38:41 Re:Re:Re:Re: Just One Night
Can-Do:
About that ring. I need it back. Urgently. Please.
=Research Scientist=

004.10:49:45 Re:Re:Re:Re:Re: Just One Night
Hi, for some reason I now have 4 copies of that ring.
-Penniless

04.11:19:26 Re:Re:Re: Hire Me
Helpless, I'm really sorry you will have to read this from the hospital. That ring was inducing a pleasure-resonance in one of your implants and you passed out while I was extracting it from your orifice.

       HandyMan
    I can fix anything

004.11:24:12 D'ohrahd Group
Do you distrust the D'ohrahd but have been afraid to speak up? You are not alone! Join a group of like-minded people who are willing to fight for freedom. We plan protests, track D'ohrahd ships, and prepare for the day when they will attempt to subjugate us.
PS Helpless Romantic: I enjoyed meeting you at the protest last night. Do you want to join our group?
       -HumanOnly-
    Live FREE or DIE A SLAVE!

004.11:30:37 Re: D'ohrahd Group
HumanOnly: Helpless is in the hospital, in case you didn't see my last post.

       HandyMan
    I can fix anything

004.11:49:09 Give Them Back

Handyman, Penniless, Can-Do, Helpless:
It looks from your posts that you all have come into contact with a very special ring. I can't go into details, but it is vitally important that you send me all copies of the rings AT ONCE.
=Research Scientist=

004.12:08:31 Re: Give Them Back
Dear Research Scientist,
I'd like to keep this ring for a while, if you don't mind. I can't identify the metal it is composed of. Can you tell me more about it?

            HandyMan
      I can fix anything

004.12:30:16 Re:Re: Give Them Back
Are you crazy? These rings are the best thing ever happened to me. WOOHOO!!!!!!!!!!
-Pennilesss but HAPPY HAPPY

004.12:51:08 Re:Re:Re: Give Them Back
keep your pants on research scientist...
why should i give up my rings unless you tell me why it's so important? i'm having quite a bit of fun with it, and i know you know what I mean.
-can-do

004.13:28:43 Re:Re:Re:Re: Give Them Back
To Handyman and the rest of you space monkeys: You have no idea what you are dealing with!! Everyone with a copy of the ring must send it to me now or there will be SERIOUS CONSEQUENCES!!
=Research Scientist=

004.13:38:02 Re:Re:Re:Re: Hire Me
handyman? yoohoo...would love to get together with you
again...u and i both know what about...
-can-do

-High Earth Orbit (HEO) Station Public Announcement-
Due to unexpected severe understaffing, service may
experience frequent interruptions.

004.15:30:55 Good God
Wow. Dragged myself out of bed to post. No longer need
food, water. Feel great. The ring is duplicating itself in my
bathtub. Splitting and splitting, like cells in the womb. I will
give copies to everyone. I will be a god. Maybe I am a god.
--Handyman---
---   Can fix stuff -------

004.17:35:17 Alien Relations?
Just got out of the hospital. I heard that one of the research
scientists at the station was arrested for having "relations" with
a D'ohrahd. Anyone else hear anything?
~Helpless Romantic

004.20:35:29 Anyone there?
Hey! No posts in four hours?! Where is everyone?
Hellooooo.....
~Helpless Romantic

004.21:47:00 Re: Anyone there?
Why didn't anyone show up at the meeting tonight?!?
                    -HumanOnly-

Live FREE or DIE A SLAVE!

004.22:50:02 Re: Good God
Handyman, You are my god. Love your bathtub.
-Penniless

-High Earth Orbit (HEO) Station Public Announcement-
If you find a ring-shaped object in your possession, do not touch it. The D'ohrahd have warned that the ring is a living being and will reproduce under humid conditions. It is also a sacred component of the D'ohrahd religion, and should be treated with the utmost respect. For humans, contact with the ring causes hallucinations, dizziness, and severe dehydration possibly leading to death.

004.23:45:10 About that Public Announcement
They forgot to mention the feelings of massive euphoria and the addictive qualities.
=Research Scientist=

004.23:47:16 Re: About that Public Announcement
Scientist- are you out of jail? So what is it? A virus? Are they trying to kill us all?!!
                    -HumanOnly-
            Live FREE or DIE A SLAVE!

004.23:48:50 Re:Re: About that Public Announcement
Obviously, you do not scan the news feeds. From HEO E-REPORTS: "...the ring-shaped object, which grows and shrinks according to its environment, is an alien organism that lives in symbiosis with the D'ohrahd in the ecosystems of their bodies. The surface proteins are intoxicants to humans and are absorbed through the skin. They will not survive away from

the D'ohrahd."
In case you did not get the point:
If you have a ring you should RETURN IT AT ONCE before
it dies!
=Research Scientist=
PS I was not "in jail". I went voluntarily to the police to
help in their investigation of the ring problem.

004.23:49:46 Re:Re:Re: About that Public Announcement
So how did you come to be in contact with this alien organism
in the first place? "Special" alien relations?
-HumanOnly-
Live FREE or DIE A SLAVE!

004.23:50:19 Re:Re:Re:Re: About that Public Announcement
You are all idiotic and rude and I will not post to this board
again.
=Research Scientist=

004.23:51:27 Re:Re:Re:Re:Re: About that Public
Announcement
Good riddance. We don't need any alien buggers here.
-HumanOnly-
Live FREE or DIE A SLAVE!

005.03:35:09 Help!
anyone:
my ring is no longer functioning properly...anyone have a
copy?! will pay!!!
-can-do

005.04:34:20 Re:Help!
Mine isn't working, either. I'm sooooo miserable.

-Penniless

-High Earth Orbit (HEO) Station Public Announcement-
The D'ohrahd have issued a public statement that they are profoundly offended by the illicit use of the ring organism at the station. They have warned that they will abandon the station and earth and never return unless the humans return all the sacred organisms at once. Please note that the organisms will die unless returned to the D'ohrahd. If you currently possess one, return it immediately to proper
authorities.

005.06:33:20 Re:Re:Help!
need ring desperately...please...anyone...
-can-do

005.07:00:42 Watch Out for Fakes
...bought a "ring" from someone claiming to have a source. Should have known better. All it did was give me a massive headache.
-Penniless

005.07:10:08 Re: Watch Out for Fakes
Thanks, Penniless. I almost acquired one of those as well. I never got to use the live ring. Sigh.
~Helpless Romantic

005.07:37:26 Fucking aliens
-can-do

005.07:44:05 Re: Fucking aliens
Exactly. That was the problem.

                HandyMan
          I can fix anything
       Specialty in ring removal

-High Earth Orbit (HEO) Station Public Announcement-
For sadness at losing our alien friends, HEO will institute a
time of e-silence and will suspend board postings for one hour
during the Goodbye Ceremony for the D'ohrahd.

005.09:11:54 Alien Departure Ceremony
Celebrate the alien departure! Speeches, music, food!
                -HumanOnly-
          Live FREE or DIE A SLAVE!

005.09:20:03 Re: Alien Departure Ceremony
Hey, sounds fun! Will there be dancing?
~Helpless Romantic

005.10:05:51 Ring Recovery Anonymous
Don't let the loss of your ring ruin your life. Please join us in a
meeting tonight to share recovery stories.

                HandyMan
          I can fix anything
       Specialty in ring removal

005.10:08:25 Re: Ring Recovery Anonymous
Hey everyone, I only got to use the ring once. Can I still come
to the group? Will there be dancing?
~Helpless Romantic

005.08:35:00 Seeking

...a ride off this miserable station. Played out, exhausted, ringless. Will do anything for a ride off-station. *Anything*.
-Penniless (once again) in High Earth Orbit

Ghosts of Bombay

Sudipa finally phoned me. Her voice was exactly the same, and she talked about Ravi and the ocean and the traffic in Bombay as if no time had passed since we last spoke. "Mitchell," she said. "I've missed you."

I closed my eyes and pressed the phone tightly against my ear, trying to shut out the sounds of the crowds and blaring horns that drifted into my apartment window from the street below.

"I'm surprised you're still in Bombay," she said. "I was sure I wouldn't reach you."

I found myself unable to reply. It was really her, the real

Sudipa. Not the ghost that had stayed with me all these years. Not the ethereal Sudipa who followed me from room to room in my small apartment, a clear and beautiful reminder of her own absence.

She talked about her cottage on Malabar Hill, where she now lived with Ravi. I cringed as she spoke; it was the cottage we should have shared, with the window overlooking the Arabian Sea and the star jasmine growing from the back door clear down to the beach.

She stopped, finally, and the silence over the line stretched on.

I forced myself to speak. "I'm still teaching at the College," I said. I walked to the window and looked down on Kasturba Street, with its multitude of vendors and tourists.

Crates of tomatoes and mangos lined the dusty sidewalks beneath strings of pale, plucked chickens and wreaths of garlic and peppers. Pedestrians and bicyclists fought for space among the cars and rickshaws. I had thought—hoped—her ghost would be gone, but there she was, weaving through the crowd with a basket of fruit and dried peas, working her way toward my apartment. The smell of sweat and dung and frying meat hung in the air like a thick fog.

"I'm glad I found you," she said, then took a breath. "I need your help."

I pulled the window shut despite the heat. The sounds of traffic were muted through the glass. "Are you all right?" I asked carefully.

She paused before answering, and I imagined her standing with the phone cradled to her ear, her hand covering her face the way she did when she was upset. "I'm all right," she said finally. "It's Ravi."

"What has he done? Has he hurt you?"

"No, it's nothing like that. It's hard to explain. Please, Mitchell. Can you come today?"

I hesitated. It wasn't far, but to see her again, after so long—I wasn't sure I was up to it. I looked at my reflection in the window. Short, bristling brown hair across my scalp and chin. Sudipa used to say she loved my eyes, pale green against dark lashes. I wondered if she'd notice the gray creeping in at my temples now, or the lines forming at the corners of my eyes.

I squinted and could almost make out Sudipa's ghost in the glass: a dark, hazy form standing behind me. As I watched the image coalesced and her face became distinct against her glistening black hair. She kissed my cheek, and I imagined I felt the feathery touch of her lips.

"Please, Mitchell," Sudipa said again. It sounded like she was crying, but I couldn't tell if she or the ghost had spoken.

I looked away. Of course I would go. She was with me every minute of the day already. "All right," I said. "I'm on my way."

*

The train to Bombay Central was packed. I squeezed in to

one of the crowded compartments as the train lurched from the station. Tobacco smoke and loud conversation swirled in the hot air around me. I was glad the trip would be less than an hour.

I glanced up to see the ghost standing at the edge of the platform, waving to me. She beckoned insistently, and I shook my head before I knew what I was doing. The man next to me stared at the empty platform, then back at me. I ignored him. I was used to it now, no longer embarrassed by the stares.

Sudipa took a few steps to keep up with the train, then swung herself up onto the car behind mine. I shook my head again, but smiled.

She was wearing the same jeans and blue cotton blouse as the day I first asked her out, so many years ago back in the States. Maybe she was trying to remind me of that day. She didn't need to, though. I wouldn't forget the way the sun streamed through the high windows of the campus cafeteria to leave strips of reflected light across the chipped Formica table tops and orange plastic chairs. The way her long black hair was pulled into a loose knot at her neck, a few silky strands escaping to rest casually against her cheek, lifting ever so slightly when she breathed. Her eyes were a startling hazel against her smooth dark skin.

She had been one of my students in the morning section of my mathematical methods class at San Francisco State University. All that semester I watched her transformation from the shy girl who sat in the back of the classroom and rarely raised her eyes to mine, to the top student who watched my lectures with rapt attention and challenged me with insightful questions. As her manner changed so did her attire, from the loose saris of her native country to the jeans and t-shirts which were the standard student uniform on the campus then.

By the end of the term she crackled with life. She engaged in conversation about everything with the same delighted intelligence, from the taste of the cappuccino at the student lounge to Gauss's law.

When she talked to me her attention was so fully on me I forgot that anyone else was there. I couldn't think about anything except her. As the teaching assistant, I wasn't allowed to ask her out; the guidelines governing student teacher relations were strict and explicit.

But the day after the semester ended I followed her to the school cafeteria.

She laughed when I asked if she would come for a ride with me up the coast. When she said yes, I didn't think I could be any happier.

We spent all that winter and half the summer at my small apartment near Golden Gate Park. In the evenings the breeze through our open windows brought the smell of the sea and the distant rumble of the waves against the shore. Nights I lay awake, listening to Sudipa's soft breath in the darkness.

It was impossible to believe it would end, though she had warned me.

"My family is searching for a suitable marriage partner for me," she told me one evening as we stood in the living room next to the window overlooking the ocean. I have no memory of the view that day, only her wide, sad eyes as she looked at me and told me she would be going back to Bombay.

"Did you tell your parents about us?" I asked.

She shook her head and turned toward the ocean. "They don't have to know."

"I'll come to India with you," I said. I tried to catch her eye, but she stared steadfastly out the window. I was finishing graduate school that year, and was certain I could find a teaching position in Bombay.

"You don't understand, Mitchell. It's already being planned."

"How can you marry someone you don't even know?"

Sudipa looked at me then, and her eyes were set with fear and determination. "If I don't do this, I'll lose everything. My community, my family. You can't understand what it's like."

"Marry me," I said. I took her hands in mine. "We have our own community, our own friends—"

"I can't simply give up what I've known all my life." Her eyes flashed with anger. "And you shouldn't ask me to."

She pushed my hands away and pulled her arms across her chest, hunching her shoulders as if against a chill wind. She rested her head against the window, and I watched the glass cloud over with her breath. Finally, without turning, she said, "You know I love you, don't you?"

I left the house without answering. When I came back later that night she was already gone.

But I was determined not to let her go so easily. I didn't really believe she would go through with it, that she wouldn't come back to me. Shortly after she left I moved to Bombay and found a temporary teaching position at St. Xaviers College.

While I struggled to understand basic Hindu and Urdu, and learned to haggle with street vendors, and grew accustomed to sweet cardamom tea in the afternoons, and became sick and then well again, and finally settled into my teaching schedule and found my way around the sprawling chaos of the city, Sudipa made her wedding arrangements and refused to see me.

The announcement arrived at the end of the summer. In beautiful gold script Sudipa's parents proudly announced the marriage of their daughter to the son of a well-known Bombay businessman. "Mitchell," Sudipa had written in small letters at the bottom of the card, "Please understand that I have to do this. It's just as hard for me."

I crumpled the announcement, walked out of my apartment, and threw it in the gutter, already overflowing with trash. Then I sat on the pavement and wept. She was wrong; it was harder for me.

Her ghost arrived the day she married Ravi. I had just stepped off the bus on Kasturba street and was five yards to my door when suddenly she was walking toward me. Her arms were outstretched in greeting, as if she had been waiting for me, perhaps watching from the window. My heart pounded happily and I stepped forward to embrace her, and then suddenly she was gone, and there was only the jabbering of the crowds and the roar of cars and the smell of burning tires and diesel fumes. Two old men in traditional red and blue Sikh turbans stared at me. I dropped my arms to my side and stared into the dusty air where she had been.

I started to feel her presence everywhere. Matching my step during my evening walks, lying on the bed next to me in the mornings. I caught glimpses of her, real enough that I found myself maneuvering to avoid her in my small apartment, squeezing past her shimmering form as she stood in the doorway to the bedroom.

At first I thought it was just a memory, manifesting itself to fill my lonely days. But I knew I wasn't imagining her ghost when she started speaking. "Did you see the precession on Navroji Street today?" she'd ask, or "I talked to your sister about her new job." She said things that surprised me because they were exactly the kinds of things Sudipa would have said, but never had. She wasn't the distant and gentle nostalgia of a memory. She was raw, unpredictable, and her eyes sparkled with laughter or darkened in anger just like the real Sudipa.

Later that winter I heard through a friend about the birth of Sudipa's first child, and then the child's sudden death. I felt her loss, though still she wouldn't speak to me.

My teaching obligation was up after that year and I could have left India then, but somehow the weeks turned into months turned into years. I settled into my strange routine of busy mornings and afternoons at the College, and evenings with the ghost. And I was seeing more of her every day. I was afraid if I went back to the States she would follow, trailing after me like the forlorn and hungry dogs that roamed the streets outside my apartment.

*

I caught a cab for the five mile journey from Bombay Central station to the cottage. The driver maneuvered skillfully between buses and cars and donkeys, alternately accelerating full speed and braking abruptly. Eventually the huge apartment complexes of the city dwindled, giving way to the quieter suburbs of Malabar Hill. The warm, salty breeze caressed my face, and I closed my eyes, breathing in the familiar smell of the sea.

The driver stopped at the end of the short gravel driveway, and I stood staring at the cottage as the dust from the taxi's passage slowly settled to the ground.

The house was one of those built during the early part of the century, an elegant two-story Victorian, with a balcony running all the way around the second floor. But as I drew closer I saw the paint was mottled with brown stains from the sea air, and there were large gaps in the wood covering the front porch.

Low, bright orange flowers grew haphazardly here and there in the front yard. As I tried to recall the name of the flowers the door swung open and Sudipa appeared. After all those years of seeing her ghost, finally I was looking at the real Sudipa again. I realized I was clenching my hands, my nails digging painfully into my palms. I forced myself to breathe slowly, to still the shaking in my limbs. I started across the uneven ground.

I had thought her ghost might disappear when I saw Sudipa again, but she appeared next to me as I walked.

I stopped in front of Sudipa. She wore a bright red sari, and her arms were covered in silver bracelets. But there were dark semi-circles under her eyes, and her mouth was drawn in a tight frown. She seemed smaller than the ghost, somehow, and I realized it was because she held herself hunched slightly forward.

So different from the ghost who stood casually with her hands in her hip pockets, taking in the house and the beach beyond.

"How have you been?" I asked. It sounded inane. I tried again. "Have you been happy?"

"What kind of question is that?" Sudipa snapped, and I almost stepped back from the forcefulness of her voice.

Then something in my face seemed to soften her. "I'm sorry," she said. "It's just—" she stopped. She twisted her hands together and stared at the wooden boards of the porch.

I reached out and pulled her carefully to me. She relaxed

in my embrace.

"Mitchell," she said, her voice muffled against my chest. "It's been so long."

I nodded against her soft hair.

Sudipa pulled away. She bit her lip, still clenching her hands together, and looked at me with wide, unblinking eyes.

"What happened, Sudipa?" I asked. "Has Ravi done something?"

"It's strange," she said. "You won't believe me."

I smiled reassuringly. Whatever it was, I was sure I had seen stranger. "Tell me."

"You knew I had a child?" When I nodded she continued, "He died in the hospital after he was born." She looked down for a moment, and I felt a rush of sorrow for her. "Ravi never got over it. He wanted a son so much. We were going to name the boy Mahesh. And then we started seeing him."

"Seeing who?" I asked, but I already knew the answer.

"Mahesh. We saw him first as a baby, then growing older, just like he would have if I hadn't—" she stopped, closed her eyes a moment. "He would just suddenly appear. Down at the market, or running on the beach. In our house was the hardest, because when we were tired and alone, we sometimes thought he was really there."

I nodded slowly and tried not to look at her own ghost standing next to me.

"Ravi became obsessed with Mahesh," Sudipa continued. "Whenever he saw Mahesh he followed him around. Finally, he did something—I don't know what—to follow Mahesh. And now he's gone. I mean he is here, but—" she faltered.

"Gone?" I tried to look past her into the dark interior of the house. "What do you mean?"

Sudipa led me through the narrow hallway to the back room. Ravi lay on a sofa against the far wall. He was thinner than I had imagined. His face was gaunt and there were dark smudges under his closed eyes. I walked over and put my face close to his, listening to his shallow breathing, then carefully pulled up an eyelid. The pupil was fully dilated, unseeing.

"He needs to go to the hospital," I said. Sudipa shook her head vigorously. "No. A hospital won't help."

I straightened up, about to argue, and caught sight of the ghost standing next to me, half smiling, as if amused. As I watched she sat next to Ravi and put her hand on his forehead.

"He has gone to search for Mahesh," Sudipa said from behind me.

I turned my back on the ghost and faced Sudipa, who was anxiously clenching her hands together. "What makes you think I can help?" I asked.

"Please, Mitchell," she said. "I didn't know who else to call."

"You expect me to bring Ravi back for you," I said. I crossed my arms across my chest. It was cruel of her to ask this of me. "Why don't you just go after him yourself?" I struggled to keep my voice low and even.

Sudipa's eyes flashed. "You said you would help." But I

could see through the anger in her eyes. She was frightened. She didn't want to go where Ravi had gone. It frightened me too, I realized, though I had been living with the ghost for years.

I shook my head. "Why do you want him back? He wanted to go. Let him stay wherever he is."

"He'll die, Mitchell. His body is still here." She stared steadily at me. "I thought I could count on you."

I clenched my jaw.

"He went to find his son," Sudipa said, her voice softer. "Wouldn't you have done the same?" She stepped forward, raising her hands in a pleading gesture.

When I didn't reply, she continued, "We haven't been able to have a child since Mahesh. He did it for me. He thought he could bring our son back." Her voice caught and she squeezed her eyes shut. Tears rolled down her face.

"Mahesh is dead," I said quietly.

Sudipa put her face in her hands and her shoulders shook as she wept. I felt the knot of anger dissolving as I watched her. Ravi wanted to meet his son. Maybe I would have done the same. I looked at Ravi's still form and wondered if I would be able to see his ghost, or Mahesh's. Sudipa's ghost still sat on the sofa, but as I looked around the room I saw no others. Only the off-white walls and the bare, tiled floor and through the window, the blue sparkling ocean.

I had thought that somehow everything would change when I saw Sudipa. That the ghost would disappear, that

Sudipa would return to me, and that we would go back to the life we once had. But here I was, finally with her again after so many years, and what I suddenly wanted was to be back in my apartment with the ghost.

I sighed. "Okay," I said. "I'll try. But I don't know if I can find him." And if I did find him, I thought, I wasn't sure I would try to bring him back. "Where did you usually see Mahesh?" I asked.

She thought for a moment. "Most often along the beach."

"Then that's where I'm going." I paused. "Sudipa, I need to be alone to do this." The truth was that I wasn't sure if what I planned would work.

But Sudipa didn't argue. "I'll wait here," she said.

*

The sky had dimmed to a dirty red, and the last of the sun's rays skimmed the wide expanse of water, lighting the wave tips briefly before escaping into the night.

I walked the shoreline, listening to the waves slap gently against the sand. The pebbles poked through my sandals. The ghost walked beside me, as I had known she would. How many times had she beckoned to me before, back in my apartment? I would follow her now, as I was sure Ravi had followed Mahesh.

I cleared my throat. "Sudipa," I said. It felt strange to be talking to the ghost. She glanced at me, but continued to walk. She had taken off her shoes and swung them by their laces as she walked, stepping lightly across the sand.

"Sudipa," I said again, and stopped walking. "Take me there," I said to her back. "Please."

She looked over her shoulder at me and smiled. The old smile. It was hard to place at once, the difference. But then I knew. It wasn't just happiness in her face, it was love. The real Sudipa hadn't smiled at me like that today. I blinked hard, and swallowed. I suddenly wanted to be part of the ghost's world. The place where she still loved me, where she had chosen me, where we had forged a life together. The need tightened around my chest and threatened to suffocate me. I stepped forward, holding out my arms, and the ghost turned, and stepped into my embrace.

And suddenly we were there.

It was abruptly daylight, and the sunlight sparkled so brightly from the water that I had to squint, and Sudipa was suddenly real in my arms. Real, warm, breathing, and holding me tightly, and then stepping back to look at me with affection. And it was real! I wanted to shout wildly and dance and run.

I was laughing and crying at the same time as I pulled her to me again and kissed her and stroked her hair back from her smiling face.

"What took you so long?" she asked with a laugh.

I looked around. We weren't in India, I realized. The houses were different, and the wind carried a familiar chill.

It took a moment to orient myself. Then I knew where I

was: back home on the California coast. So she had stayed with me, after all. It was so close, I realized. This reality, half a world away but existing right on top of the other. I had passed from one to the other without even moving.

I looked around again, and a movement from the rocks out in the surf caught my eye. I stared, making out a small figure.

"Go get Mahesh," Sudipa said, kissing me lightly on the cheek, "before the tide strands him out there. I'll unpack our lunch." She started up the beach.

I watched her walk away. Was this really what would have happened, I wondered, or a dream? The sand under my feet was hot, the cry of the gulls shrill in the wind. I shook my head. It wasn't a dream. I started toward the figure on the rocks. The cold water reached my knees, soaking my sandals and my trousers, but I didn't care.

I didn't see Ravi until I had climbed up the small island of rocks and crouched next to the boy. Ravi squatted further down on the rocks, looking out across the ocean.

He turned when he heard me, and his eyes narrowed. "Are you the father?" he demanded.

The boy looked up at me from the shell he was holding, his green eyes sparkling with happiness. "Look, a conch!" he said, holding out the shell to me. His hair was rich and dark, like Sudipa's. But his eyes were mine.

Ravi stood up and started toward me. His form rippled strangely, as if made of water.

"You don't belong here," I said.

"He doesn't belong here," Ravi answered, pointing at the boy. But his voice had lost its edge and he stopped moving toward me.

"Go back to your world," I said. "Mahesh stays here."

"My world," Ravi echoed, his voice soft. He slumped his shoulders. He was growing fainter; already I could see the ocean through him. "You're right. Mahesh wouldn't have fit in there."

I realized what he meant. Mahesh the green-eyed boy would have been an embarrassment to Ravi. I thought of something Sudipa had said. That she and Ravi couldn't have children. So Mahesh was mine, in both this world and the other. Only here, he had not died after he was born. I felt the cold wind bite through my shirt, though the sun still reflected brightly from the water surrounding me.

"Why did she do it?" Ravi asked. But he wasn't looking at me anymore; he seemed to be talking to himself.

"She loved me before she met you," I said. I had imagined saying that to Ravi many times. In my fantasies it was vindictive and gratifying. But now it just seemed cruel. I almost felt sorry for him.

Ravi shook his head sadly, and disappeared.

A voice called from across the water. I looked up to see Sudipa waving from the shore.

"This isn't what happened," I said. Mahesh looked up at me, uncomprehending. "It's what I wanted to happen," I said. I took a last look at the waves splashing against the rocks, the sun coruscating from the water, Mahesh's dark head bent in concentration once more over his find.

And then I simply let go. It was so easy, because I knew the other place had been right there on top of me all along.

*

I opened my eyes to darkness. The sand and pebbles were warm against my back where I lay, and the sound of the waves lapping against the beach whispered in my ears. I raised myself up shakily.

"Mitchell," a voice called. I made out the figure of Sudipa, running from the house.

"Thank you, Mitchell," she said, catching her breath. "Ravi's all right. He woke up."

I tried to discern her expression as my eyes adjusted to the weak light.

"Are you all right?" she asked finally, when I didn't speak.

"I'm okay," I said, my voice hoarse. Then I asked, "Sudipa, was Mahesh my son?"

She was silent. That was answer enough, but then I felt her hand on my arm. "Yes," she said.

"How did he die?" I could barely hear my own voice, but I couldn't stop myself. The years were falling around me like a thunderous waterfall, cascading me back to the Spring when I read that Sudipa's child had died. Now I understood what had really happened.

The hand was gone from my arm, and Sudipa's angry voice reached across the years and pulled me forcefully back to the present. "What are you implying, Mitch? How could you think such a thing?"

Before, I would have reached out to reassure her, to calm her. I had been swept along with Sudipa's moods, like a branch caught in a strong current. But now all I felt was a strange hollowness.

You didn't have to kill him, I wanted to say. But I didn't. It was over and done, and I wanted nothing more than to leave Sudipa's house and her sad past.

I watched her for a moment, her arms wrapped around her chest protectively, pulling her shoulders forward. She narrowed her eyes as she stared back, but her gaze was flat, the anger dulled with resignation. It was hard to believe I had once seen those eyes crackling with anger or wide with delight.

I turned and started up toward the driveway, and she didn't follow.

At the place where the gravel path met the main road, I paused and looked back toward the ocean, a dark mass barely visible in the moonlight. The wind was colder now, and I suddenly wished I had brought a sweater. But I knew by the time I reached the city the sun would be rising. And in the warm morning air the ocean would sparkle a deep blue, and the small flowers growing determinedly from the sandy soil would open up, their orange and red petals like tiny fires dotting the ground. Nasturias, I remembered, half turning to say the name aloud, then realized no one was beside me.

I looked around, startled. The air around me was strangely empty. No other presence. Only the soft whispering of the wind and the faint smell of lemon grass. The ghost was gone.

I lifted my head and breathed in deeply, letting the cool night air fill my lungs. I would start to pack when I got back to the city. It was time to go back to the States.

Just me, with no ghosts trailing behind.

I smiled and started the long walk back toward the station

The Great Marriage

The house wore wooden siding and rested comfortably on its concrete base. Its screen door squeaked open a fraction and then closed again.

"Is this your house?" I asked the man standing next to me. He was tall, with a red beard and round eyeglasses.

"No," he said. "Yours?"

"No." But the house felt familiar.

The screen door banged open and a young man bounded through. He took the front steps two at a time. He carried a large canvas pack. He grinned at us.

"Off we go then," he said.

Without waiting for either of us to respond, he hurried down the trail that led away from the house. The forest crowded against both sides of the trail, pines or some kind of conifer, with ferns and brush packed tightly between the trunks.

The young man's boots kicked up dust and hung in the air, obscuring his receding figure. Further in the distance the forest appeared to converge onto the trail, closing it off completely.

I suddenly realized that I didn't know where I was, and I had been aware of this lack of knowledge for some time. The house, I thought, was the key.

I ascended the steps to the door. The screen door hung open, and there was no inner door. When I looked back at the tall red-bearded man, he was scowling and watching the receding figure of the young man.

I stepped inside. The house consisted of one large room with a scuffed wooden floor and four dusty windows, one in each wall. A table squatted in the center of the room, bearing a line of canvas backpacks. Behind the backpacks were an assortment of items: round flat tins, squares of fabric, metal tools for some purpose I could not discern.

The door opened behind me and the red-bearded man stepped through. Red, I thought, would be a good name for him. The color of both his hair and his mood. He went immediately to the backpacks and opened one.

I followed and opened another. The pack was empty.

Red picked up one of the cans and pulled the tab on the top. Inside was a white substance, reminiscent of tuna. Red sniffed it, then picked up a chunk and tasted it.

"Chicken," he said. "Or maybe fish." He shrugged. "Food for the journey."

"Where are we going?" I asked.

"*We* aren't going anywhere," he said. "*You* are on your own."

He began picking up the cans and putting them in his pack.

I picked up several and put them in my pack as well.

He squinted at my backpack. "You need all those?"

I was suddenly aware of the difference in our sizes.

"Yes." I gripped the straps of the pack and pulled it toward me.

He hesitated. I waited.

Finally, he turned his attention back to the other items on the table.

I picked up one of the pieces of fabric. It appeared to be a simple woolen square.

Red picked up a knife, several metal hooks that might have been fishhooks, and a pen.

"I bet that guy took all the good stuff," he said. He went to one of the windows and peered out. "Not much daylight left."

I didn't want to stay in the house with Red, but I also didn't want to be wandering the forest at night.

I sat on the floor with my pack. I put the square of wool on my lap, then realized it was more than just a single sheet. I peeled one layer from another; they were connected. I found that it could be unfolded again. Four times, five times. Now it was large enough to be a blanket.

I draped the material over my legs and leaned back against the wall. The makeshift blanket was much warmer than I had anticipated. But I didn't want to fall asleep.

The bright lights of an oncoming car blind me for a moment, and I squeeze the steering wheel tighter.

The terror of the dream woke me. I had slid partially down the wall. I realized I was hearing an intermittent patter and shush. When I looked out the window I could see the rain falling against silver backlit clouds.

Another sound drew my attention: a yelp from outside on the porch. I scrambled to my feet.

"Don't let it in." Red's voice came from a dark bundle in the corner.

"What is it?" I said.

Red didn't answer.

I went to the door. The yelp came again, plaintive.

I opened the door a crack. Hopeful eyes stared up at me over a silver muzzle. The creature was fox-sized, with gray and white patches along its flank.

"It's just a lost dog," I said. I opened the door to let it in.

The poor thing was soaked. He walked in, shivering. Water dripped from his fur and pooled at his feet.

"I told you not to let him in." Red was standing now. He came out of the shadows and stood in the middle of the room. "Put him out."

"But he's cold."

"He'll want to eat all our food."

I looked at the dog. He did look skinny. "I can give him some of mine."

Red took a step closer. "If you can spare food for him, you might as well give that food to me."

I looked from Red to the dog. I imagined putting the dog out and shutting the door. I imagined going back to my corner and trying to sleep. Outside it would be cold and wet. Outside I might get lost.

I felt the breeze pushing the smell of rain and pine into the house.

"I'll get my pack," I said.

The porch was narrow and offered meager shelter from the rain. Besides, I didn't like that Red was inside, with an inexplicably bad attitude toward both me and the dog.

I unfolded the blanket and raised it above my head, then stepped off the porch. The dog followed close by my side. Droplets splashed on the material and slid off the side in small rivulets.

To one side of the trail the sky was dark. On the other side, twilight. It didn't seem closer to night than when I had entered the house. Perhaps I hadn't been asleep very long.

"To the trees, then?" I said to the dog.

He followed when I splashed through the puddles and mud to the side of the trail on the lighter side. The bracken was matted down from the rain, and the going was easier than I had anticipated. Water dripped from the leaves and branches. It was darker in the forest than on the trail. I could just see the dog's eyes glint as he turned his head to look into the depths between the trees.

We worked our way for a while through the wet plant life, and then a small clearing opened up ahead of us. Sparse light shone down, enough to see a circle of moss around a large tree.

I leaned the pack against the tree and spread the blanket next to it. I sat on it, and the dog came to me and settled against my leg. He was still shivering. I pulled the blanket up and around us.

There was warmth coming from the blanket. I wondered what kind of material this could be, that it could remain warm for so long. It appeared to wick away the water as well. I put my hand on the dog's side, and his fur felt silky and nearly dry where the blanket touched it.

An almost-memory came to me: cuddled in bed, a warm furry creature on one side, someone on the other side, her hand on my shoulder. Love and warmth and safety. When and where, I thought. And who? Perhaps it had been a dream.

I watched the pine branches lift and fall in a slow dance,

water dripping their resin smell into the soft air.

The dog breathed deeply, relaxed against my leg. A cricket sang out and was answered by a friend. I thought: this is a tiny moment, and lifetimes are made of tiny moments.

It's just one weekend, she says.

The bright lights of an oncoming car blind me for a moment, and I squeeze the steering wheel tighter.

I hate these country roads, I say. I hate this drive.

He's a lonely old man, she says. And I don't ask you to go with me on these visits very often.

When I opened my eyes, I knew some time had passed. The light that made its way through the branches shone a bit brighter and bluer.

The dog was awake. He sneezed, then stood up and shook himself. He made a sound somewhere between a bark and a yelp.

"Is that good morning?" I asked him.

He looked at me with trusting dog eyes.

"You made a yipping sound. Is that your name. Yip?"

He made the sound again.

"So it is then," I said.

His coat was completely dry and clean. He looked healthy, though skinny. I rummaged in the pack and pulled out one of the tins. I pulled the tab on the top, picked up one of the pale chunks inside, and tasted it. Not tuna, but definitely food of some sort. It could have been a very mild fish, or chicken, or ground chickpeas.

"Not bad," I said. I pulled a chunk from the can and put it on the ground at Yip's feet. He sniffed it, then carefully picked it up with his teeth, tossed it to the back of his mouth and swallowed. He looked at me expectantly.

A dog is like a smile, I thought, and had to smile at the image. Always ready to laugh, to trust, to enjoy.

I put the remaining chunks at his feet and watched him eagerly lap up the food.

Long fronds of ferns shiny with water bent close to the ground, continuing to drip, though the rain had stopped. A bird darted in a flurry of yellow through the branches above, and came to rest not far away, eyeing us. He fluted out a complex descending scale and was answered by a distant friend, the same tune.

I pulled up the blanket and shook it, then folded it back into its impossibly small size. I placed it in the pack. When I stooped to pick up the can, it was gone. I looked at Yip, but he was nosing in a cluster of ferns not far away.

I looked up at the bird, which turned its head back and forth to look at me from one eye and then the other.

"All right, then," I said. Yip looked at me. "Ready to go?"

As if he understood, he trotted into the trees.

He wasn't heading back to the trail but continuing the way we had come last night. I followed.

I expected to be stiff from sleeping on the ground, but my

limbs felt refreshingly limber. Even my knees appeared up to the task of walking on the uneven surface, sending out not one complaint at the sudden activity.

We broke free of the forest within an hour.

The sky was clear of clouds, though when I looked back from where we had come, the sky over the trees was dark.

In the other direction, grasslands rolled into the distance, where purple mountains peeked above the horizon. I knew those mountains were my destination.

As if in answer to my decision, my eyes caught sight of a trail off to my left, emerging from the forest and winding the hilly contours into the distance, eventually merging into the narrow purple at the horizon.

I paused and set down my pack. I didn't need to open it to know that there were four tins left. That was not enough food for the journey. Maybe Red had been right. But then I thought: even if I had his five tins, it would still not be enough.

Yip trotted ahead, then came back again and circled my legs. He gazed up at me with his wise dog eyes.

"Not much choice about it," I said. "We go on."

I shouldered the pack and continued forward, angling to converge with the trail in the distance. Yip bounded ahead.

Perhaps I could find wild berries or roots. Perhaps there would be a stream where I could fish. Though of course I had no fishing gear with me, and no means to build a fire. Perhaps I would starve.

The ground was soft beneath my feet, the going fast.

Before long I had stepped onto the trail, which turned out to be finely crushed rock in shades of orange and brown.

I looked back toward the forest, and my heart sank at the sight of a figure emerging from the trees. Even at this distance I could see it was Red, his tall figure slightly stooped as he strode forward.

I started forward again, picking up my pace. He would steal my food, I thought, take my blanket. Hopefully that would be all.

I looked back and he was closer. I tried to walk faster, but it was no use. He was faster than me.

Nothing to do but stand and face him, I thought.

I turned and stood waiting. Yip bounded back to me and leaned against my legs. He began to tremble. I reached a hand down to stroke his head and calm him.

Red stopped when he was ten or so feet away. He glared at me from behind his round spectacles. Beads of sweat stood out on his forehead.

"Thought you could just run away?" he said, the challenge clear in his voice.

"No," I said.

"Give me your food."

I removed my pack and set it at my feet. "I have four tins," I said. "It won't be enough for you, even combined with yours."

He narrowed his eyes.

Reason would not work with him. I noticed then how thin

he was, his collarbone jutting from below his neck. I saw the sweat beaded on his forehead. I saw the tense set of his jaw.

I also knew that he would never be gone from me. That I must reconcile, or forever live in fear of him.

"You're frightened," I said, and knew it was true. "I am, too."

His jaw relaxed a fraction. He looked past me toward the mountains, then down at Yip, and finally back up at me.

"I'll give you my food and then we can part ways," I said.

"We can't part ways," he said gruffly. "We have to go the same direction."

"Why?"

"Can't you see it? The dark?" He looked back the way he had come.

Indeed, the clouds were more densely packed now over the forest, blocking out the light. The trail drained to black only a short way into the trees.

"The damn grass got stiffer, too," he said. "Couldn't walk on it without hurting my feet."

I nodded, feeling it somehow made sense. I shouldered my pack and he did the same.

"All my life," he said, "Everyone else got what they wanted, and I was left out."

I nodded, listening.

"My older brother always got my father's attention. Better, stronger, faster than me. Always."

"He was older," I said.

"Yes," Red said. He shrugged. "I guess at that age it can make a difference."

"And later?"

"The same. He went to a better college, was better at sports."

"You felt it wasn't fair."

"Damn right."

"It doesn't sound fair," I said.

"He got to have a dog. I didn't."

"Definitely not fair," I said, looking at Yip. The dog had stopped leaning against my legs. He was working his way closer to Red, looking up at his face as he did so.

I suddenly saw past Red's anger to its source, the jealousy and hurt and fear which were all more difficult to bear than the anger.

"It must have hurt," I said.

"See here," he said. He pulled up his shirt, and I saw it: a long red wound, as if from a sword, not healed, but pulling apart at the edges, beginning to reveal the vulnerable flesh beneath it.

I looked at his wound and felt his pain. I looked at his eyes and saw tears there.

Now Yip leaned against his legs.

"I think there's a medical station past those mountains," he said. He pulled his shirt down over the wound.

"Then that's where we need to go," I said.

He nodded.

"You can manage?"

"I guess so," he said.

He seemed less angry. I realized that looking at his wound had changed me, too. I knew what suffering was like. I knew what it was like to have a wound. I knew pain. And now I saw that pain so easily blossoms to anger, and that anger is the flower above ground, bright and red and visible for the world to see. The roots of pain are hidden while they nourish the red display. But someday the flower would fade. It wasn't the only part of the plant, only the most visible.

We began to walk, shoulder to shoulder, towards the distant mountains.

Just a weekend visit once or twice a year, she says. That's all I ask.

When she gets angry, she gets quiet. When I get angry, I get loud.

What do you owe him? I'm pressing it now. I feel my own anger ballooning large and red in my chest. It presses everything else away.

Don't ruin this whole weekend, she says.

It's already ruined, I say.

I was worried about food, but there was no point in talking about it. Talking about it wouldn't change the fact that we didn't have enough.

The sky grew marginally brighter as we walked, though

the distant purple mountains didn't seem to get any closer.

The grasses on either side of the trail gave way to reeds and marsh, and I caught sight of dark glossy birds darting among the cattails, a flash of red in their wings as they swooped and danced or hung precariously to a swaying reed. Their song filled the day with beauty.

I became aware that a figure was approaching us from the gray depths at the feet of the distant mountains.

I looked over at Red, and he at me. He straightened his back as if preparing for an attack and watched with intense focus as the figure solidified into the form of the young man we had seen burst from the house.

He wasn't grinning anymore, but his step was still energetic, his eyes bright. He was wiry, but moved quickly and looked all about him, as if to take it all in.

Yip came to stand between me and Red, facing the young man.

"Well hello again," the young man said once we were within talking distance.

"Hold it right there," Red said.

Yip barked once.

"It's okay," I said. "I don't think he wants to hurt us."

"He might try to take our food."

At that, the wiry young man laughed. "Haven't you noticed that you don't need food here?" he said. He looked at us with a smile.

"What is that supposed to mean?" Red said.

"Just what it means," he said. "I don't play with words. I say what I mean."

"What's your name?" I said.

He tilted his head, as if considering the sky. "I think it might be…Earnest."

"Earnest," I repeated.

Yip sat at my feet, calmer.

The young man considered for a moment, then nodded. "Yes, I like it. Earnest it is."

"Did you come from those mountains?" Red said, his voice still gruff.

At that, Earnest's smile disappeared. "Yes," he said. "And we can't get through. It's all a lie."

"What's all a lie?" I said.

"This!" Earnest indicated the trail and the marsh and the sky with a sweep of his arm. "You think you can understand it all, make sense of it. I started out with honest inquiry. That should give answers. I have all the right tools."

He tossed his pack on the ground and out tumbled magnifying lenses, notebooks, scales and other scientific devices.

"But for what use?" he said. "I still don't understand this world. I went to the end of the forest and back, and to those mountains and back. The forest gets darker and darker, and I think there is a wall there, but it is impossible to see clearly. And the other direction—" he gestured toward the purple mountains. "It is very light but there is another unscalable wall. I can't get through or over. It's no use."

I felt sad for him. All that traveling, and no result.

"Maybe the journey was worth it," I suggested.

He sighed. "I don't understand anything here."

"You understand a lot," I said.

Both he and Red looked at me.

"You can talk and ask questions. You can move around and explore. You can hear bird song and enjoy it, and the sun on your face and the wind in your hair and the smell of rain."

"You're mixing up enjoyment with understanding," he said. "But you're right. There is joy in exploring, in seeking to understand. In the inquiry itself. But you're wrong about one thing." His smile was back.

"What's that?"

"There is no sun in the sky."

I looked up and around, and for the first time, saw that there was no source of the light. The sky was a light blue, and a few small clouds drifted over the purple mountains in the distance, but there was no bright shining star in the sky.

"Maybe it's about to rise," I said, though we could all see that the sky was brighter than it should have been at dawn.

"Indeed, it is about to rise," Earnest said.

I looked at him.

"When I got to the wall over there," he said, gesturing ahead on the trail, "there was a brightness beyond it. Bright enough to be the sun."

"You're saying the sun is trapped behind the wall?" Red

said.

Earnest shrugged. "It appears that way."

"That doesn't make any sense," I said.

"No," he agreed. "It doesn't. None of it does, really. But that doesn't stop me from trying to make sense of it."

"It's not fair," Red said. "We're just thrown in here, for no reason, and the world doesn't make any sense."

Earnest shrugged.

"There's nothing to do but go on," I said, and was surprised when neither of them argued with me.

I left my pack on the ground next to Earnest's pack and began to walk. Yip bounded ahead. I caught up to the young man and looked back to see Red hurrying to catch up. He had left his pack behind as well.

The three of us walked together, and the trail was wide enough to walk abreast.

"It seems we are meant to go to those mountains," Red said.

I agreed, though I didn't know why I should agree.

"There are all sorts of wildlife here," Earnest said. "I saw evidence of raccoons and deer and other mammals. And large predators, too. And insects and fish in the rivers. And if you like plants, there are all sorts from every Phyla and Genus—"

"Oh, be quiet," Red said.

I laughed, then looked quickly at Earnest, but he didn't seem offended. "I could stay here forever exploring," he said. Then his face grew serious. "But I think our time here is almost up."

I felt sadness then. It was a joy to explore and learn. To think. To be. But I knew that those distant mountains would be the end of our journey.

And so we continued on.

You can wallow in anger all weekend if you want, she says.

I am not wallowing.

A tiny smile lifts the corner of her mouth.

Damn it all! I say, but the words lack the force I intend.

I want to wallow, I say.

Fine, she says. We'll find a nice pond for you.

A smile is trying to work its way onto my face.

I would just rather spend the weekend alone with you, I say.

I know, she says, serious now. Me too. She looks at me, and I look at her, my beautiful spouse.

Earnest was right about the food. When I thought of lunch, as I did a few times, I didn't feel any pangs of hunger, or really any desire to stop and rest. Maybe I hadn't needed food in the morning. Maybe I hadn't needed sleep, either. Maybe it was just the habit of a lifetime, continuing into this strange place, this in-between-place, that was neither dawn nor dusk, hot nor cold.

Yip bounded ahead and then back, with no apparent lack

of energy. I even saw Red smile once or twice at the eager dog.

The scenery changed again, from marsh to brush and then to a dry forest, with inviting paths through shady groves. I could smell pine in the air and imagined sitting beneath one of those trees on the bed of pine needles and allowing myself to daydream while listening to the breeze rustle the branches high above.

A sudden cry broke my peaceful fantasy.

I looked to either side but couldn't make out anyone in the shadows of the trees.

The cry came again, from somewhere within the trees to the side of the trail.

Red leapt suddenly into the forest and ran. I started to follow, but just as quickly as he had left, Red came back, his figure appearing suddenly from between two trees. He wasn't alone. He was carrying a child.

The child gripped his neck tightly, her head buried in his chest.

"Boars!" Red said when he reached the trail. "There were wild boars attacking this child!" He tried to set the child down, but she clung tightly to him.

"How interesting," Earnest said. "I didn't see any boars in my explorations into the forests."

I gave Earnest a sharp look before turning my attention to the child. Her hair was matted, her arms covered in scratches and dirt.

"Honey?" I said. I put a tentative hand on her shoulder. "We're going to help you. You're safe now."

She turned her head slightly to look at me. Her eyes were wide. Tears streaked clean lines down her cheeks through accumulated grime.

"What's your name?" I asked in a soft voice.

Her lips trembled.

Yip stood up on his hind legs and licked the girl's ankle. She pulled her legs higher, out of his reach.

"It's okay," I said. "You don't need to talk now. We can talk later. We're going on a trip. Do you want to go with us?"

She nodded once.

"Can you walk?"

She clung even tighter to Red.

I looked at Red.

"I can carry her," he said.

"Off we go then!" Earnest said and began walking. "Boars. Imagine that."

"There's something wrong with that man," Red said.

"He's all curiosity and no compassion," I said. "That's why he needs us." I looked at Red. He was all anger and no curiosity. And his anger had served the girl well. Maybe we needed Red as well.

Yip continued his darting ahead and then back, letting out his signature single bark every now and again. When he came close, I saw that the girl was beginning to watch him. She wiggled a bit in Red's arms, settled herself again.

When Yip came back for perhaps the fifth time, she wiggled herself free. Red set her on the ground, and she ran after Yip as he ran ahead.

Finally, the mountains seemed closer. The sky was brighter as well.

Yip rounded a curve, the girl close on his heels. They were gone for a moment, and then both came running back.

"Water!" she exclaimed.

"Where?" I said.

"Just ahead."

She ran ahead again.

When the rest of us had rounded the corner, we saw that indeed a stream wound its way close to the trail there, splashing and burbling its way toward the trail and then happily away.

The girl and Yip were already in the water, splashing about.

"How about we clean you up?" I said, smiling at the girl.

She didn't seem pleased about the idea, but she came over to me, and let me wet a cloth and clean the dirt from her arms and legs and face.

"That's better," I said.

Now that she was relaxed I could see she was a pretty child, all smiles and sparkling eyes.

"How did you get to be alone in the forest?" I asked.

Her brow furrowed. "Don't know," she said.

"We should probably get going," Earnest said. He looked

up the road. The mountains did seem closer than ever now. I could make out the foothills and at first glance, what seemed to be a solid white cloud between two peaks of purple.

"That's the wall," he said.

We all looked, even Yip and the girl. The wall rose up behind the mountains, up all the way to the sky where it became a bright white band across the sky. When I tried to make my eyes follow it to the top, I felt dizzy, like I might fall over backwards.

"You can't get through?" Red said.

"You'll see," Earnest said.

We all began to walk again, and this time the girl took my hand.

The forest petered out, giving way to fine sand, lightly rippled as if the land were a vast ocean.

"Do you have a name?" I asked the girl.

"It's the same as your name," she said.

"All right," I said. And then had a moment of panic as I realized I didn't know my own name.

"That's how I feel," Red said, looking at me. "Can't remember my own name." He shook his head, clearly angry at himself.

"Earnest knew his name," I said.

"I think Earnest gave himself the name Earnest."

I suspected Red was right.

I felt a bit of fear, then. Maybe Red felt it, too, because he walked closer to me. The girl gripped my hand tightly, and even Earnest came back to walk closer to us, though still in front, and still with a bouncy step. Yip circled our group, sniffing the sand on each side, then back around again, as if to convince himself that it was the same on all sides.

The mountains grew large against the white backdrop of the wall.

As we got closer still, I could see that the trail wound between two low boulders on either side.

We were at the boulders before I could think about it and walking between them.

"Into the Shadow of the Valley of—" Earnest started.

"Stop it," Red said. "You'll frighten the kid."

She did hold my hand tighter as we walked into the shadow of the giant granite boulders, which now appeared to be pillars. Past them, the path curved to the right, and then back again to the left, and then straightened out, ending in a solid white wall.

"See?" Earnest said.

He reached the wall before the rest of us and laid a hand on its surface.

When I stepped close, I could see it was completely featureless. It went up and to the left and right as far as we could see.

I pulled my hand away, and the others did the same. In unison, we looked up. The light was blinding at the top, and we had to look away.

We, I thought. Red and Earnest and the girl and Yip all

stood very close to me now. Red's shoulder touched mine, and then merged into mine. Yip leaned against my legs and then was gone. But I could feel him inside me, his little eager heart and adventuresome spirit and trusting nature, bringing out the compassion in me. The girl, too, held tight to my leg and then disappeared. I felt her naivety and simple-hearted fear and joy, so easily squashed or abused, but still alive within me, after all these years. Important to take care of those aspects, I thought. Earnest was the last, but he merged easily, too. I appreciated the nature of inquiry, the need to question and explore. I was complete again, and now I was ready.

"It's not a solid boundary," I said to the Earnest inside me. "It's just that once you cross through, you can't come back."

So what are we waiting for? Earnest-me said. Let's go see what's on the other side.

Indeed, my hand was beginning to sink into the wall.

Wait, the little girl inside me said. Yes wait, Red echoed. One more thing.

Yes, I thought. I had one more thing to do before I crossed over.

*

I open my eyes to sunlight. The blinds are wide open.

I remember that I once said to my beautiful spouse, If I am ever dying in a hospital room, please do not keep the blinds closed; I want to die in sunlight.

My spouse sits on an orange chair, a book in her lap and a box of Kleenex on the arm of the chair. Crumpled tissues cover her lap.

She looks up at me and then stands so quickly that the book drops with a hard clunk to the floor and all the tissues scatter. "You're awake!" She moves to the bed and leans in close, and now I can see the tear-spattered glasses, the dark circles under her eyes.

"They said you wouldn't wake up," she says. "They said it was too much damage. They said—" but she can't speak any more. She takes my hand and buries her face on my arm.

I can see the IV trailing from my arm, hear the soft blip of the heart monitor. The sheet has an odd pattern on it, and she grips it into folds, hiding the checkerboard pattern. My limbs feel very heavy and my neck is so stiff that I know I couldn't lift my head if I wanted to. But I also know this is temporary. All of it.

"Did you get hurt?" I manage, my voice barely audible despite my effort.

She shakes her head, then picks up a cup I hadn't noticed on the tray beside the bed. She pulls the small sponge from a plastic cup and wets my lips with it.

"They said I was incredibly lucky," she said. "The car was totaled. But I don't feel lucky."

"I'm sorry," I say. "I wanted to spend the weekend with you."

"Shhh," she says. "We can talk later."

She doesn't understand. This is the last chance we will ever have to talk.

"There is no later," I say. "I'm going to die."

"No, you're not," she says firmly. "Not any more. It was touch-and-go for a while. That's what they said, touch-and-go, but now…" She trails off and looks at me.

I look at her, and because of our years of marriage, because we have known each other through anger and laughter, and depression and joy and jealousy, and all the variations in between, and because we have talked throughout the journey together, because we have been angry and selfish before and forgiven each other, because of all this, I know that she knows I am telling the truth.

"I was being selfish," I say. "I'm sorry that I let my anger endanger us."

"It's not your fault," she says softly. "The other driver went into our lane."

"Still," I say.

"We all make mistakes," she says.

And now I feel my own tears. She is forgiving me, and I am leaving her.

"I need to tell you something," I say. "I had the most amazing dream and I wanted to tell you."

She looks as if she is about to argue, but then slowly nods.

So I tell her about my incredible journey to that in-between land. I tell her about encountering Red and being afraid, but that his anger was necessary to save the girl. About Earnest and his determination to understand everything, about the trusting love of Yip.

When I tell her about the wall that I will have to pass through very soon, she begins to cry anew. I realize I don't need to tell her anymore of it, because she already understands.

She understands that very few people are just one thing, all anger or bluster or goodness or selfishness or altruism or inquiry, and that the point is to see all of it and bring it all together within yourself, and to try to help other people do the same, because in the end we are all on the same journey.

I squeeze her hand one last time.

I head through the wall to the other side.

Acknowledgments and a few story notes

Thanks to my spouse, my family, my friends and writing colleagues who have helped me through the years become a better writer and a better person. You have given me loving support when I was dispirited, helpful critique when I was losing perspective, and companionship along this road of life. Many of the stories in this collection were read first by fellow writers in critique groups, and this feedback often helped make the stories better. Thanks also to the magazine editors who first accepted and published these stories. Finding an acceptance note in the inbox is like discovering an orange ring buoy when you are drowning in a sea of rejections. You writers out there know what I am talking about.

The story "Quantum Entanglement" remains one of my personal favorites. Quantum physics gives us perfect metaphors for exploring the human experience, which I also find strange, beautiful, and mostly incomprehensible. Writing this story felt like I was dredging up strange equations from somewhere within that only barely made sense at the time. Years later, I can see more clearly that the story is part autobiographical, and that has helped me understand the relationships in my own family. Similarly, both the "The Giving Heart" and "Looking Back" were written at at time when I was in a relationship that wasn't right for me, but which I couldn't quite see at the time. Writing those stories felt like standing very close to a mirror and trying to describe all the tiny details of the image without understanding how all those details added up to a larger picture, if only I were able to step back for a moment. "Faith is a Nanooka" was inspired by one of my all time favorite books, Life of Pi. In that book, Pi tells a fantastical story of his survival at sea with a Bengal tiger. Then, when pressed, he tells an alternate story of survival at sea with a murderer. In both stories, the outcome is the same. He asks, "…which is the better story, the story with animals or the story without animals?" While believeing a story doesn't make it true, it can make it true *to us*. "All Things Are Full of Gods" is dedicated to Inkey, a wild crow who was my best friend in sixth grade. Yes, I was a strange kid. "This Side of Kinsey" pokes fun at how fixated our society is on secondary sex characteristics and how we tie those characteristics to arbitrary societal ideals of beauty and clothing. And who knows, maybe someday we will in fact be able to change our twenty-third chromosome completely so that XY becomes XX or vice-versa, or possibly even add in a third strand of DNA and become something else entirely. "The Sound of Science" was written for a short story contest set at a scientific facility called a synchrotron, and I am proud to say I won first place in that contest. It probably helped that I actually work at a synchrotron facility and so was able to get a lot of setting details right, though of course the story veers from the start into complete speculation. Finally, "The Great Marriage" is both my tribute and my challenge to C.S. Lewis's novel, "The Great Divorce."